Five Worthy Souls

David B. Ahern

ISBN: 978-0-646-89776-9
Copyright David Ahern June 2024

The characters in this book are fictional and any resemblance to anyone living or deceased is purely coincidental. They are the creation of the author's vivid imagination.

To Michael and Philip

Chapter 1
Whitechapel
Thursday 30 August 1888

The English summer was coming to an end. Another summer that had failed to deliver. Cold with the occasional flooding rains, the warmth of past summers had vacated much of England. For the thousands of Londoners who flocked to the seaside for their annual holiday with a fair expectation of sunshine and heat, the weather didn't come to the party. Describing the recent summer, the banner headline on one Fleet Street newspaper simply said:

Miserable.

But for London's East End, home to almost one million people, the weather played little part in their lives as each day was much like every other day. No summer vacation for these folk; many of them immigrants from Ireland and Russia; many of them poor. Rain or shine, most days were like a trade fair. The streets were clogged with horses and carts and hordes of people trudging through their daily chores. Animals of all shapes and sizes ... chickens, pigs, goats, dogs and cats. A menagerie.

No one cared. No one noticed. The noise and the chaos were part and parcel of their livelihoods. As was the filth, dirt and disease that beset their communities.

Few of the residents were well-dressed. The tone was set by the scruffy, their clothes no more than rags. This wasn't Kensington or Mayfair. No well-to-do ladies and gents and their hoity-toity manners in this part of the city. The hour was early. People were out and about; many were inebriated, and many had one thing in mind. Either looking for fun or plying an age-old trade to make ends meet. The neighbourhood did not discriminate, catering for all kinds.

Now after one in the morning, the woman was exceedingly annoyed that she'd been forced into the darkness and the cold to find the money for her night lodgings. The absolute gall of the housekeeper. That she'd demanded four pennies for a bed was outrageous. Surely, the money exchange could have waited until the morning. Who the bloody hell did she think she was? Some people had no consideration, believing they could bully the likes of her because of her profession; because of her misfortune, and where she grew up.

Well, she wasn't about to be bullied. Bugger the housekeeper and bugger her family!

Ordered from the Thrawl Street premises, the woman replied sarcastically that she'd soon have the money, even if it meant finding a man for a bit of slap and tickle. For many years that had been her living. And she'd done just fine by it. She straightened the long bow of her black bonnet under her chin and draped the shawl around her petite shoulders. Her cheeks were unpowdered. Comfortably middle aged and a mother of five, she could still gain a man's attention, especially where sex was involved. She plied her trade well. That men found her attractive was heartening and raised her spirits whenever she was down.

And there were many days she was down.

She pushed her breasts up just enough to show some cleavage. The men had to be suitably aroused and she'd had enough practice to know what succeeded. Her breasts and her figure worked for her.

Time to get to work.

Leaving the lodgings, the woman made her way down Osborn Street. Now after two in the morning, she was becoming increasingly bothered at her predicament. Hard going. The bloody drink had taken its toll and her walk was now more of a stagger. Stumbling a few times, her tatty leather boots were well-worn, the stitching starting to split. There was a need for new boots, but the money wasn't there.

Gas lamps were infrequent along Whitechapel's labyrinth of roads, courtyards and alleyways, making for dark and dangerous conditions. Even for locals who knew their way around. Few Londoners travelled to Whitechapel, particularly at night.

Most of the local men had had their fill of beer and women so finding four shillings for sex at this time of night could be a challenge. She only needed four pennies for a bed, but she wouldn't lower her standards. It was four shillings and that was final. She continued towards Whitechapel Road which was only a short walk and where she believed she'd have more luck. But the men seemed drunker than her, staggering and laughing at their own lewd jokes. In raised voices they spoke dirty as she passed.

Delighting in their crude suggestions, they yelled, "Show us what you've got" and "I'll bet you're tight."

A reaction was their objective, but they got none. Her silence was her victory. There'd be no satisfaction from these drunkards on this night. Bastards. On she walked, eventually spotting a man of youthful stature leaning against a brick wall. The nearby streetlamp cast enough light that she could make out his disposition. The clothes were always a good sign of a man's character.

Handsome he was. Well-dressed he was. He'd do.

Standing alone, he wore a feathered black felt hat and a long, dark coat with a fur-trimmed collar. His clipped, carroty moustache curled at the ends. Not much taller than herself, though at 5 feet two inches she was hardly big in stature. He gripped a long cane in his left hand which he was lightly striking on the cobbled road as if waiting for someone, impatiently.

The woman's cheap gaze found its mark. His frown was barely visible. Unwelcoming. She didn't notice. Luck at last, she decided, as she eagerly approached. Her mouth remained shut as she didn't want the stranger to notice her missing front teeth. Surely, he'd be put off. Besides, her breasts were her selling point. The gap in her mouth did not affect her performance. She could do all the tricks. But to avoid the indignity of the missing teeth, she'd learnt to speak like a ventriloquist with her lips barely parting.

"Allo deary," "Lookin' for fun ... are we? The woman's words were slightly slurred, but she wasn't about to hold back. The hour was late and lodgings for the night were her priority.

Only silence. The stranger pointed his cane at a stable gate across the road.

The woman took that for an aye and slapped his hand. Lightly. "Don't be shy. Four shillings ain't much. You needin' company."

The rickety gate was hanging precariously on its hinges, the woman pushing it open, hurriedly. Her intentions were clear. Almost tripping, she slumped against a side wall temporarily halting her fall. She knew the drill. The quicker the better. In one rapid movement, she yanked her dress above her thighs. She'd been on her feet for many hours. Drowsy, her bones ached for a bed to rest, but first the paying customer had to be satisfied.

And satisfy him she would.

"Git it out then. Not a one woman show ... it ain't." She drunkenly giggled. Though the hour was late and she was tiring fast, she could still manage a laugh.

The man was quick to raise his arm, the knife invisible to her intoxicated eyes. The blade slashed her throat. Imperceptibly. There was a faint shriek as the knife sliced her skin. Deeply. Twice more her throat was ripped by the blade. There was a thud. Losing consciousness, the woman slipped down the wall to the ground, helped along by a solid push. Cataleptic to the frenzied attack, her abdomen and vagina were brutalised with the sharp instrument.

Soon, her body was still.

No one witnessed the cruel attack. Called Polly by her friends, she was found on her back with her dress almost above her waist. Her bonnet had slipped from her head and was on the ground next to her body. In the days and months ahead, the locals would agree that Buck's Row in London's East End had never witnessed such carnage. A heinous crime. It was unfathomable than anyone could die in such a manner, even in one of London's rougher areas.

The unfortunate soul stood no chance. The man who committed the crime was labelled a monster.

Chapter 2
Adelaide Australia
Present Day

Henry Evans pushed the toast from one side of the plate to the other. Crumbs sprayed over the table but there was no attempt to clean them up. As his partner walked into the kitchen, he remained focussed on the toast. He did not look up.

"Morning dear. You're up early for a Saturday. Couldn't sleep?" said Claire, who loved early mornings, especially on weekends. She was very spritely on this day. Though late August and still officially winter, the forecast was for a warm, cloudless day, and no wind. After seeing the weather report the night before, Claire undertook to get up even earlier.

"Morning ... sleep wasn't great," said Henry, acknowledging his partner. "The past two nights have been average."

"That's no good. Why?"

"Bad dream actually. Strange stuff. I can't recall having a nightmare since I don't know when." Henry kept poking the toast with his finger, creating even more mess.

Sitting, Claire held Henry's hand. "You, okay?"

"I'm fine. Just trying to remember the details of the dream. A woman was murdered. Not just killed but her body was diced and sliced." Almost gagging, Henry pushed the plate and the half-eaten toast to the centre of the table.

"How dreadful, Henry ... no one we know I trust!" Claire grimaced. "If it was Mrs Jones next door I wouldn't mind so much. She's such a pain. Always complaining about how much noise the kids make. Seriously, they're children."

Henry didn't react to Claire's attempt to lift the mood as he considered the more macabre elements of the dream. "No. I can barely remember the woman's face or that of her attacker, but the assault was so vivid."

"You're working too hard. It's Saturday and you need to relax. It's going to be a nice day. Let's go for a long walk at the beach, Glenelg or Henley. We can soak up the sunshine with the kids. They may even want to swim. It will be a fun day out for the family!"

Henry nodded, agreeably.

Childhood sweethearts, Henry and Claire had dated from their mid-teens when they were still at school. Not exactly love at first sight but there was an attraction. Claire liked Henry's kind heart and desire to help people and Henry was captivated by Claire's longing to improve the environment. After completing her final year exams, Claire spent a year backpacking with a girlfriend through Europe, much to Henry's disappointment. Not that Henry would've had much time for her as his nose was to the grindstone finishing his first year of medical studies.

He was a self-enforced workhorse.

After being together for more than twenty years, they were still very much connected to one another,

neither imagining they could ever have another partner. Parents to three children, two girls and a boy,
they'd considered a fourth child but opted for a dog
instead. Three kids and a dog were enough. Claire, having an interest in minerals and rocks, was a part-time
university lecturer in Geoscience. Whenever she told
people what she did their faces would blank over. Not
a profession that everyone could fully comprehend or
take to, but alongside Henry, it was Claire's first love.
Concerned about climate change, understanding the
past, she believed, could help solve future problems.

Weekday mornings during the school term created unnecessary tension in the home. All three children
made Claire's life hellish. Disorganisation and tardiness
were hallmarks of the younger members of the family.
Claire had the job of dropping them off at school, but
fortunately they all attended the same school ten minutes' drive away.

Could have been so much worse. Different schools?
Different drop off times? Claire would've had trouble
coping.

Brushing a strand of hair from her eye, Claire reluctantly let go of Henry's hand. She left the kitchen
fully believing overwork was the cause of Henry's acute
tiredness. He'd been a GP for a decade but the onset
of the Covid pandemic had at times made life almost
intolerable. His suburban practice had been busier
than ever, and 14-hour days were not uncommon. He
would leave by seven in the morning and often not get
home until after eight in the evening. His day wouldn't
end there. After a quick supper, he would work until

ten at night. Most Saturdays Henry put in another four hours at his medical practice.

Today was an exception. There would be no extra hours. His family would come first.

Now almost bald after enjoying a full head of hair until his early thirties, Claire put it down to stress, overlooking the fact Henry's father also lost his hair at an early age. Something had to give, and Claire was concerned Henry's mental state could be seriously affected if he didn't slow down. Many doctors were expert at imparting advice but not so good at being counselled about their own ailments.

A common joke amongst medical professionals. A truism if ever there was one.

Henry wondered why the dream so bothered him. Only a dream. Yet, it was the viciousness and the gory detail of the attack that so disturbed. The knife slicing across the woman's throat and the gushing blood. Remorseless. He had kept the more gruesome aspects of the murder from Claire, like the woman's dismemberment, her vagina being cut, the mutilation of her abdomen and her bowel protruding from her body. The images were as clear as the toast on the table.

Henry had to pull himself together.

He had come from a long line of doctors starting with his great-great-grandfather. They'd excelled in the profession and Henry fortuitously had inherited the family business and a desire to help others. They had worked hard and had never shown mental fatigue. Never. Or so he believed. It was a fucking dream! He had dealt with many bloody cases in real life but not the bogeyman in the middle of the night. The children had to deal with scary monsters in their dreams. Not him! He and Claire were present for the kid's bad dreams; Harriet, 13, Lucy, 10 and John, 6.

Claire was on the money. A relaxing day at the beach was the tonic for the sorrow he had for the nameless woman who was murdered. A woman he'd never met. The woman in his dream. A dose of Vitamin D was also what doctor Henry prescribed for the family. The beach it would be. Soon departing the kitchen, the toast was abandoned on the table surrounded by an ocean of crumbs, Henry not thinking to clean the mess.

They only lived ten minutes' drive from Henley Beach, a seaside suburb that was popular with locals. An easy drive. Considering the time of year and far from the summer peak, there was a good turnout at the beach. Very few adults were swimming as the water was still too cold, but the children had no such qualms. They were running in and out of the water at regular intervals. And being a winter's day, UV radiation and sunburn were not a problem. It was one less issue for Henry and Claire to concern themselves with as there was no need to smother the kids with sunscreen.

Lucy and John, like their mother, were strawberry blonde. A day at the beach and John's hair would turn more golden blonde, making his sisters envious. What he disliked intensely was his freckled nose which became even frecklier after a day in the sun. Harriet had caramel brown hair but had longed wished for flaxen colouring like her brother and sister, believing her shading lacked lustre. She often used the word crummy to describe her hair, much to the amusement of the others.

Any family outing had to include Freddy, the Silky Terrier, the sixth member of the family. The children always insisted that Freddy accompany them on each excursion, no matter where they went. Being the eldest children, Harriet and Lucy had responsibility for Freddy on day outings, while Claire did the fair share of walking during the week. Daily combing of his coat was also Claire's weekday chore, though that job fell to Harriet on the weekends.

While an adorable and much-loved family pet, the care and upkeep were nonstop, Henry deciding if he had had his time over again, veterinary science would have been his go-to job. The cost of visiting the vet, even for a check-up, was astronomical. Not that Henry begrudged vets their weekly wage. More envy than jealousy at play.

Freddy enjoyed the water as much as the children, so a trip to the beach was always going to be a success. As irritable and stroppy children were every parent's worst nightmare, by late afternoon Henry and Claire were waiting for the arguments to begin. They didn't have to wait long; spot fires were soon breaking out on the sand. The kids were bickering over silly things. Lucy and Harriet were fighting over who should mind Freddy while John was crying after developing a stomach rash from his boogie board. Five hours at the beach had taken its toll.

Time to head home.

Freddy was first in the door, flopping into his wicker basket in the hallway, his head soon resting on the blanket. With Freddy settled for the night, the rest of the family made for the kitchen. The cavernous yawns were a tell-tale sign that sleep would come easily for the two youngest, Lucy and John. After an assortment of cheese and tomato toasted sandwiches and then brushing their teeth, they dragged themselves off to bed. No urging or gentle prompts from mum and dad were required. So tired was John, he didn't even want a book read to him. Harriet made her intentions known; Saturday night for her would be a rom-com in bed, her favourite movie genre.

Also dog-tired, Henry and Claire settled for a glass of wine on the backyard patio grateful their tired, tetchy kids had volunteered for an early night. The beach, Claire and Henry determined, would figure more prominently in family outings over summer. A healthy way to exhaust the children. Anything to make their lives easier.

Now that it was almost spring, Henry and Claire planned to use the recently constructed decking at the back of the house as much as possible. Shaded by a large gum tree, the patio would be a godsend for entertaining family and friends in the warmer weather and they looked forward to the months ahead.

Leaning back in his cane chair, Henry sipped the last of his red. "Decision time. Will I have one more drink or get an early night?"

"It's only eight-thirty, dear," said Claire, "If you have another, then so shall I."

Claire could see Henry was jaded, the dark rings under his eyes ample proof that he needed to apply the brakes and give his body time to recover. If only he were willing to take advice but no: he was a doctor and knew what was best. There were times his superior mindset rankled. Understanding his dedication to his patients, Claire believed Henry had to be more faithful to himself. He wasn't superhuman.

"You're right. One more it is." Henry reached for the half-empty bottle of shiraz and poured a hearty glass.

Claire tipped a more frugal measure of Pinot into her glass. "Have you had any more thoughts about your dream last night, darling?"

"Not really. It was so intense. Like I was there, witnessing the crime. The faces were a blur but the ferocity of the wounds to the woman ... I can't describe. She didn't scream. The attack was so sudden."

"I know you won't like my suggestion but if you could reduce your number of patients and get in a few early nights. That may help."

Knowing it was coming from a good place, Henry considered Claire's suggestion, but the number of ill people was rising. If Covid wasn't bad enough, the flu season was reaching its peak. There would be no let up for months. If only! Hospitals and general practices were desperately trying to cope with the influx of patients. It was the modern world and Adelaide was no different to the bigger cities like Melbourne and Sydney.

It was tough on everyone. Doctors, nurses and paramedics all carried an unfair burden, but they were dealing with the worst pandemic since the Spanish flu.

"Thank you, Claire. I know you're being a good friend. I'll see what I can do but no promises." Henry sipped his red. It had been a most pleasurable outing with his family and to end the day with a few drinks with his partner capped it off.

Henry raised his glass. "May there be more days like today. Cheers."

"Cheers," Claire repeated.

They clinked glasses. Following their children's example, they agreed on an early night. While the children swam and played on the sand, Henry and Claire, each with a book in hand, had hardly shifted from their beach chairs. But a day out in the fresh air was always going to be tiring. Fatigue had swept over them, so they drank the last of their wine and went indoors.

Spitalfields
Saturday 8 September 1888

The man was insistent but not angry. He towered over the woman as he spoke, his demeanour remaining calm but inflexible. "You can't have a bed unless you pay the fourpence owing."

The woman wasn't about to give up her bed for the night. "Been poorly, I 'ave. In the infirmary, you see." The woman was slightly tipsy. "I'll be back ... don't let the bed. I'll be back," she repeated, with some urgency.

The man stood firm. If you can't pay, you can't stay. Simple as that ... and you've been drinking again. I can smell it on your breath."

"Don't drink much now. On the straight and narrow I 'ave," the woman said, crossly. "I'll get the money. You'll see."

The woman left the lodging house and headed along Dorset Street. She'd get the dosh and be back in no time. A common problem finding the money for a bed. This was not the first time she'd been told no money, no bed. Her diminutive five-foot figure gave people the impression she was a pushover. She wasn't. Her health, however, was poorly as the tuberculosis had taken hold and the coughing fits were worsening, notably in the cool night air. Her friends kept advising her to stay home at night. But how could she? She had to work. The night was her office.

As she approached Hanbury Street there was a gent not twenty feet away and on her side of the street. Well-attired, he was wearing a long coat and dark felt hat. Her optimism grew. She could be back at the lodging house and sleeping in a warm bed within the hour.

"All alone dear. Company, you want?" The woman was not going to waste too much time on pleasantries. She had been combing the streets for several hours to collect the money for the bed without much luck, but her prospects had improved.

The man was tapping a long cane intermittently on the cobblestone bricks. He remained silent. The street was otherwise empty; no one else as far as the eye could see. The early morning air had freshened even further, and her coughing was now more evident.

"Only four shillings ... that's all, love," said the woman, between stifled coughs.

The woman was unsuspecting as she pulled her dress above her knees. The man held her chin and slashed her throat from left to right. Violently. Shocked, by the time she'd realised what was happening she was already losing consciousness. As she dropped to the ground, blood was spurting from the deep wound to her throat.

For the next half-hour the stranger went about his nefarious work. The time of day was on his side. Undisturbed, he cut deeper and deeper into the woman's body. Chopping rather than slicing. No care was shown. He had little regard for these types. What they got is what they deserved.

Around six in the morning, an elderly resident of 29 Hanbury Street who lived on the third floor with his family went into the backyard. The sight that greeted him would forever haunt. There lay the mutilated body of a woman lying between the steps and the fence.

Hardly recognisable as human. More like a butchered pig at a slaughterhouse.

Like the first victim, Annie had been disembowelled. Flesh from her stomach was placed on her left shoulder and other bits of flesh, as well as her small intestines, were found above her right shoulder. Part of her uterus and bladder were missing.

Upon seeing the woman's disfigured body, the resident was violently ill.

Henry woke with a start. More of a forceful jolt as he sat; the dream was still fresh. Another murdered soul. Eviscerated like the first woman.

Saliva was dripping down his chin onto his bare chest. Drying the spittle with his hankie and careful not to wake Claire, he went to the ensuite bathroom where he rinsed his eyes with cold water. They were red and angry. Why suddenly the nightmares? What the fuck was going on? He'd never had such vividly, awful dreams. Yes, he was a doctor and he had performed operations. He'd taken people's tonsils out and done appendectomies. But this? Maybe Claire was right. Slow down and take time off. The workload was too much.

After towelling his face lightly, he went downstairs.

Henry made a coffee and sat at the kitchen table. The nightmare. The appalling manner in which the woman was done in. He remembered the knife and the killer, whose face was indefinable, cutting her up as if she were a lab rat.

So barbaric!

He recalled the conversation the woman had with the man before she embarked on her mission for the night. Her inability to pay for a bed, like the woman in his first dream. And her name. Had the lodger mentioned her by name? If so, what was it? Henry racked his brain: Amelia, Angel, Audrey. If only he could remember!

Claire appeared by his side, breaking his concentration. "Morning, Henry."

"Morning."

"Dare I ask but did you sleep well?"

Henry shook his head. "Another nightmare. Another dead woman."

While Claire accepted the first dream as just one of those things, the revelation of another bad dream shocked. While she put the dreams down to Henry over doing it, there was a tipping point.

"I haven't given you all the details, Claire, but these women haven't just been murdered. They've been brutalised, horribly dismembered ... and I've been witness to every ghastly detail."

Claire stared at Henry; her words were gentle. "We need to address this Henry before it goes on any longer. I'm not sure what's going on, but you need to see someone."

Henry was about to speak up but buttoned his lip.

"It may be as simple as taking a week off. I know there are sick people everywhere but you're not exactly thriving yourself. Enough now." Claire's tone was sterner.

"I hear you, Claire. I'll arrange something first thing Monday. I promise."

Henry's unexpected surrender came as a surprise. Usually quite stubborn about such matters, Claire determined that the dreams were troubling him. Satisfied Henry was finally listening, Claire left to check on the children. Her motherly instincts kicked in; the lack of noise was strangely unsettling. What mischief were they up to? Or was she just being overly suspicious?

Either way she'd soon have an answer.

Henry finished his coffee and went to his office. Switching on the laptop, he began to google. The women he'd seen were dressed in what looked like 19th century garb. The surroundings didn't look like Australia, more somewhere in Europe or the United Kingdom. He began by googling notorious brutal murders. He typed in words such as eviscerated, disembowelled and gutted. As a doctor he was well accustomed to such language. His search soon pinpointed 19th century London and the name, Jack the Ripper.

Henry read about the infamous slayings that had plagued London's East End in the late 1880s. There were numerous killings but many of the records concentrated on the deaths of five women, the so called canonical victims: Mary Ann Nichols, Annie Chapman, Elizabeth Stride, Catherine Eddowes and Mary Jane Kelly.

They were alcoholic prostitutes who lived in a slummy part of London and had trouble making ends meet. While they lived more than 100 years earlier, Henry couldn't help but feel immense sadness at what these poor wretches went through. Many had to flee abusive husbands or boyfriends who liked nothing more than to dish out a beating after a night on the grog. No wonder they were forced into prostitution. How else could they live? Then there was the question of their children. How were they to survive? Life was a nightmare in 19th century England unless you were part of the privileged middle and upper classes.

Why else did the English transport so many convicts to Australia? Their prisons were overflowing, and the 'scum' of the earth had to be sent somewhere. While convict transportation had well and truly stopped by the 1880s, England, like many countries, still had its law-and-order issues.

The poverty that racked the nation was also at the core of its crime problem.

So, there it was. The name Annie Chapman, the Ripper's probable second victim. But were these the women he dreamt about? He re-read the circumstances around the deaths of Mary Ann Nichols and Annie Chapman and couldn't believe the parallels in his dreams. He knew of Jack the Ripper. It was a name synonymous with evil. But not being a history buff, he was positive he had never watched a documentary or read an article about the Ripper murders. Not in any detail anyway. The interest factor was zilch. Nature documentaries were his go. The David Attenborough docos were a big favourite.

Henry browsed the horrific particulars around the death of Annie Chapman one more time and was now certain her murder was what he'd seen in his dream. After reading the graphic description of her evisceration, he closed the laptop feeling sickened.

While it was almost lunchtime, Henry wasn't hungry.

Chapter 3
Whitechapel
Sunday 30 September 1888

The woman always tried to look her best when she went out, irrespective of whether she was on the job. This night was no different. Wearing a black jacket and skirt, complemented by a black crêpe bonnet, the evening began drinking with a friend at the Queen's Head pub in Commercial Street. But it was only to be a brief catch up, and after a short conversation and a drink they went their separate ways.

Now down to other matters.

The woman had been turning tricks for many years and knew her way around men. In the more than twenty years since arriving in London from Sweden, she had been married and divorced. With curly, dark brown hair and a pale complexion, finding a man was never a problem. But a turbulent relationship with her current boyfriend meant there were nights she had to find alternative accommodation. Of late she'd been residing at lodgings in Flower and Dean Street.

Lack of money was rarely a problem. In addition to her night-time trade, she did housework at local residences to top up her weekly earnings.

There had been several clients before midnight, men of a charming discourse. Some males were no fuss;

get it over and done with while others wanted to talk beforehand. No judgement here as it was all about the money. And as long as she saw the dosh upfront there was little likelihood of a row. Having a calm deportment, anxiety over money was displeasing.

Now approaching one in the morning, she thought she'd try her luck one more time before retiring for the night. When luck was on your side you had to go with the flow. There were nights when finding a man was like trying to catch fish in the Sahara Desert. Then there were nights when the men were as plentiful as the stars in the sky.

The International Working Men's Educational Club in Berner Street was often a good place to trawl for male company. Knowing this area well, many of the gents were Jewish businessmen with money to spend. They had more money than they could spend in one night. So trawl she would.

The man in the long black coat was almost upon her before she noticed him. He approached quietly and from the opposite direction. The cane in his hand was unmissable. As was the hat with the single black feather. She wasn't about to criticise his dress sense, but the feather seemed out of place.

The woman leant against a wall and eyed him closely. "How are ... you sir ... this fine night?" she asked. She had a slight stutter as a result of an injury received to her mouth in a shipping mishap years earlier.

The man didn't speak. He signalled with his cane for her to follow him into nearby Dutfield's Yard. Poorly lit, the woman didn't hesitate but because of difficulty seeing where she was stepping, walked slowly. Ten feet into the yard, she was sprawled on the ground after being shoved from behind.

"Aye. Steady on ... You'll get it."

As the woman tried to stand the blade sliced her neck. The pain was instant, blood pouring from the single wound. As she took her last breath, the stranger plotted his evil act. Her right arm was placed over her stomach and her legs were drawn up with her feet almost touching a side wall.

The stranger was about to get to work on the body when he was disturbed by a noise in the yard. Believing someone was close by, he made a hasty exit onto Berner Street. The job was incomplete. He was furious.

Whitechapel
Sunday 30 September 1888

The woman could have taken a quicker route back to the Flower and Dean Street lodging house in Spitalfields, but instead of taking the shortest way home and turning right after leaving the police station, she turned left towards Aldgate.

There was a man she'd planned to meet who could assist with her enquiries. Or so she believed.

Earlier in the night she'd spent a few hours in a cell at the Bishopsgate Police Station after being discovered drunk on the street. Not for the first time had she been in a lock up. Never a pleasant experience but it came with being a drinker and passing out, usually at an untimely hour. The bobbies were always around to make a tidy arrest. Some were pleasant while many were ghastly. But she reasoned they had to earn their money somehow. The constable on this occasion had been reasonable enough saying she would be released once she sobered up. Initially worried she'd be locked up all night, at one in the morning she was told she could go.

Thank Christ!

The woman had planned to meet a man in Mitre Square so being held in a police cell overnight was not part of the plan. She hadn't mentioned it to the police but had told friends she had a fair idea who Jack the Ripper was. Not that she was believed. Her friends thought it fanciful. On her part. While no reward had yet been offered for the killer's capture, the woman was hopeful that such information could result in a payment.

Even a small sum would come in handy.

She longed for a healthier lifestyle where prostitution played no part in her life. Orphaned at the age of fifteen after both parents had died, she valued her independence. Only five feet tall with wavy auburn hair, she was invariably described by friends as a jolly woman who had a fierce temper. Not that she would admit to it, but close associates had told her she indeed had an uncontrollable rage.

If you crossed her, watch out!

The woman approached the entrance to Church Passage, a narrow walkway that led to Mitre Square. A man, leaning on a cane, was standing at the entrance. A few inches taller than her slight build, he had a moustache that curled at the ends while his head was covered by a dark felt hat.

The laneway was otherwise deserted.

"Michael?" she asked, tentatively.

The man didn't speak. He twirled the end of his moustache.

"You 'ave news about the Ripper. There's a dear. Speak up ... 'aven't got all night."

The man's hand was swift. The woman was caught off-guard. Her bonnet slipped to the back of her head as her body buckled unexpectedly, the sharp incision to her throat causing an abrupt and massive bleed. The pain stunned. Her throat was on fire. Now numb to what was happening, soon her heart would stop beating.

No time to waste. The stranger jerked her clothes up above her thigh and began to cut into her stomach. With precision. The stranger didn't pause for a second. He was meticulous; dogged. The woman's intestines were drawn from her body and placed over her right shoulder. A piece of intestine was then extracted and placed between the body and the left arm.

Job done. The knife vanished inside the stranger's coat, and he fled the square on foot, taking the same route he'd journeyed along Church Passage not twenty minutes earlier.

Upon the discovery of the woman's body, the high pitch shrill of a police whistle was heard. The short, sharp sounds echoed throughout the square, piercing the otherwise still night. A former copper had stumbled upon the body and immediately whistled for assistance, a serving policeman soon answering the alarm.

While on the scene within minutes, there was no one to arrest. The stranger had long made good his escape, blood still oozing from the many wounds to Catherine's body.

Henry shouted.

Her throat had been cut from ear-to-ear. Horrific injuries had been inflicted on the woman. Part of her intestine had been cut from her body and put on her shoulder. What a madman! Who could do such a thing? Inexplicable callousness.

Frightened by Henry's night terror, Claire sat upright and fumbled for the switch to the bedside lamp.

"Another dream, darling?"

Henry nodded. Bile was steadily rising in his throat. Sitting in bed, the woman's repulsive death was recalled in every minute detail. It was as bad, if not worse than the other killings.

Henry and Claire, despite the early hour, made for the kitchen. Both needed a warm drink, milk or cup of tea, to soothe their growing unease. They could go back to bed and still get plenty of sleep. There was no need to get up early as it was Sunday.

They quietly sipped their teas with little communication. Henry continued to recreate every small detail in his head. The stranger's face was a blur, but his black hat and cane were clearly identifiable. The man's wardrobe was identical every time. And typical of the Victorian era, the woman wore a bonnet.

A narrow laneway leading into a large square. That much he could recall.

"Fuck."

Henry's expletive caught Claire by surprise. He rarely swore as he wanted to set a good example around the children. While the kids were presumably tucked up in their respective beds the swear word startled, Claire's eyebrows furrowed.

"I saw another woman murdered tonight," said Henry.

"I know. That's why we're down here drinking tea at two in the morning."

"There were two killings in the dream I just had. The murderer struck twice."

"Could have been the same woman but from a different angle?" Claire knew the comment made little sense but then Henry's dreams were not making much sense.

But Henry was adamant. "No. They were two separate killings."

Henry left the kitchen and walked briskly to his office, Claire feeling the need to follow. He logged onto his laptop and found the original Jack the Ripper site where he'd gleaned the earlier information.

Resting a hand on his shoulder, Claire stood behind Henry.

While he had read about the deaths of Mary Ann Nichols and Annie Chapman, the facts around the murders of Elizabeth Stride and Catherine Eddowes were unknown to him. He checked the dates of their deaths and found they'd both been killed on the same night, 30 September 1888. The circumstances around their deaths were similar, but while Eddowes was butchered like the others, Stride was relatively untouched. There was no mutilation.

Police reports put it down to the killer being interrupted during the attack.

Henry kept reading about the Eddowes' murder in Mitre Square. He had seen a square and a laneway in his latest nightmare. The woman had been talking to a man before he slashed her with a knife and proceeded to cut her open.

It had to be Eddowes.

"This is remarkable, Claire. Not only am I seeing their horrific injuries, but the murders in the order they occurred. How can that be?"

"I really can't say Henry, but you need to seek help. This is getting way out of hand."

Henry had yet to deliver on his promise to Claire to seek professional help. He understood her deep concern and was willing to follow through, but his workload had been intolerable in recent weeks. Where would he find the time?

Claire wouldn't accept too many more of his excuses. That much he understood.

Freddy's flap door was useful in case he had to relieve himself or have a run in the backyard. Henry and Claire believed the doggy flap door was one of the best inventions ever. Rather than having their pet bark or scratch the door down to be let out, Freddy could move in and out of the house without pestering the family.

Day or night.

The flap door was most welcome in the middle of the night, though on the odd occasion Freddy had barked incessantly at the possums, prompting a stern warning from Henry who had to go downstairs and fetch him. The neighbours were friendly, except Mrs Jones, but no one appreciated a barking dog in the early hours as it would test the patience of even the most temperate.

The noise was faint, but it was loud enough for Henry to stir. The digital clock on his bedside table put the time at one minute after three in the morning.

Claire was sleeping soundly. While the night was now still, it sounded like Freddy, but Henry couldn't be certain. About to roll over and go back to sleep, nature was calling so he went to the bathroom. Because he was already up, Henry decided to go downstairs and have a look. A quick circuit of the house wouldn't hurt. Henry reached the hallway, but the wicker basket was empty.

Perhaps it was Freddy's bark that caused him to wake. Bugger. He'd have to go to the back door and call him. It wasn't a warm night and Henry was only wearing underpants. There had been many a night when he had found himself at the back door calling for Freddy. As adorable as Freddy was, these nightly shenanigans were painful.

One of the downsides of having a dog.

Henry unchained the back door and stood, momentarily. Searching hard into the darkness, he couldn't see Freddy. He waved his hand in front of the sensor that was attached to the back of the house and the light came on.

Whispering, he said, "Freddy, here boy?"

Still no response. This was becoming frustrating. And he was only dressed in his undies.

"Freddy, where are you?" This time Henry said it with more verve.

Henry walked to the back lawn for a better look. The frosty grass was brisk on his feet. He should've put slippers on, but it was too late now to concern himself with a missed opportunity. Freddy wasn't anywhere to be seen, but Henry would walk around the side of the house to double check. A sensor light was also fixed to the side wall to avoid wayward tumbles in the dark. It was times like these he was glad they'd spent the extra money on a second light.

Henry crossed the lawn and soon reached the side of the house where a narrow-pebbled path wound its way to the front garden. He walked ten steps when ...

"What the fuck!"

The yell was as loud as any dog bark. Gooey intestines squished under Henry's feet and oozed between his toes. Henry had stepped on Freddy. Well, what was left of him. Bloody bits covered the path. His head was hanging by a thread.

Henry screamed again. "Fuck!"

Claire scrambled to find the lamp switch. "Henry, what's up?"

"Freddy's dead. Mutilated by a sadist. Fuck, the poor dog. The kids ... they'll be distraught."

"You were dreaming, Henry. Freddy's not dead." Claire cradled Henry. "It was another nightmare. Take a few deep breaths." He was as white as their bedsheet. Rambling, he was still not quite awake.

"I tell you, Freddy is dead. At the side of the house. Some sick bastard has taken a knife to him. Cut him into pieces."

"No darling, you were dreaming. Let's go downstairs and check on Freddy."

Claire had her nightgown on before Henry had one foot off the mattress. Walking to his side of the bed, she helped him to his feet. "Come on, dear. Let's see how Freddy is."

"He's dead. I saw him, Claire. Disgusting. How could anyone do that to our pet?" Henry couldn't remember how he came back to bed. The last thing he saw was Freddy's body at the side of the house. That Freddy was dead, however, was not in question.

Claire led Henry down the stairs, holding him by the hand. When they reached the hallway, to their utter dismay, the wicker basket was empty.

"I told you. Freddy's gone. He's around the side ... in bits."

They stood at the empty basket, Claire now wondering if Henry hadn't been dreaming. They were about to check the other rooms when there was a noise upstairs. Henry and Claire climbed the staircase, first reaching Harriet's bedroom. They peaked through the partially open door, but she was asleep. The next room was John's. He was also dead to the world, with his blankets strewn across the floor and his torso almost touching the carpet. It was such an odd angle to find their youngest asleep. Claire gathered the blankets and lifted John back into bed. She tightly tucked him in before she and Henry went to Lucy's room.

The door creaked as it opened. They approached Lucy's bed. She was also fast asleep with an angelic face that brought smiles to their faces. Both later acknowledged such precious imageries reinforced the unconditional love they had for their children. Still holding hands, Henry and Claire were about to leave when there was movement in Lucy's bed.

"What's that?" said Claire, squeezing Henry's hand.

"What's what?"

"The blanket is moving."

Claire pulled back Lucy's top blanket. Freddy's wet snout appeared; his eyes charmingly wide. He looked pleased to see them, his tail wagging under the blanket. "Oh Freddy, you shouldn't be up here. Come on, back to your basket." Claire gave Freddy a helping hand as he leapt from the bed. "All good, Henry. See, it was just a dream."

Confused, Henry said, "I could've sworn it was real. I was outside and … honestly, Claire I saw Freddy dead at the side of the house."

"Back to bed, Henry. Freddy is alive and there's nothing to concern yourself with."

Closing Lucy's door, Claire watched Freddy scamper downstairs to his basket. If only Freddy had known that he wasn't in trouble.

Henry and Claire were just happy to see him.

Chapter 4

Aldgate

Tuesday 15 May 1888

Bertha Eckersley sat at the old oak desk. She reached for a dip pen from the top drawer along with the leather-bound journal that was gifted to her by a cousin. She loved writing. Her mother taught her cursive at a young age. Each letter had to be joined and the flow had to be flawless. Writing, for Bertha, was akin to poetry in motion.

One of her greatest offerings to her only child, Bertha would be forever grateful to her beautiful mother who had long since departed the world. The words were never rushed, Bertha first constructing the sentences in her head before putting pen to paper. Every word had to be carefully pondered. She began slowly, deliberately. No need to rush.

Bertha, a stocky woman with green eyes and light brown hair tied back in a bun, began to write. On this day her log would not be a happy one.

'Another strange occurrence yesterday. Unfortunately, they are becoming all too frequent. I prepared supper for Aldrich when he arrived home at 7 p.m. However, he wasn't interested in eating. It wasn't like him. He complained of a headache and went to bed. I didn't hear from him for the remainder of the night.

As we live in separate bedrooms, I have little idea how he slept or the state of his mind. By the time I was up this morning he had left for work. I do worry so about Aldrich. I can only assume he's having difficulties at work, but he refuses to say. A stubborn man if ever there was one. On occasions he makes me feel wretched and so miserable.'

Bertha revisited each word that she'd penned. A shorter entry than usual and pained by what she'd written, the journal was closed and placed under a thick wad of papers in the top drawer of her desk.

With any luck tomorrow's entry would be brighter. That was her considered hope.

Married for ten years after meeting in their early twenties, Bertha prayed each day her marriage to Aldrich would survive another year. But there were days like the one just gone that triggered serious doubts.

Henry was in a frightful mood. He had misplaced a patient's file and despite rifling through the drawers of his desk and searching almost every room of the house, the papers were nowhere to be found. How could he have been so careless? As if the recent dreams weren't enough, the last thing he wanted was to fuel his anxiety by being bloody clumsy. He should've been at the clinic twenty minutes earlier, but the missing file had to be located. The patient was booked in for an appointment that afternoon.

Henry often didn't record his notes correctly. The files on his laptop were not always updated with the annotations that he would jot down on a writing pad. It was not for the first time that he was in a bind of his own making.

"Fuck this." Henry's expletive was so loud it prompted Freddy to leave his wicker basket and scurry into the office.

"It's all right Freddy. I'm fine. Just pissed off with myself." Henry did not consider for a moment that his choleric temperament would not be understood by Freddy. As if he were addressing one of his children, he said, "It has to be here somewhere Freddy, but where? I'm sure I left it on my desk. Perhaps it's in the car."

Freddy's tail wagged. Happy with the situation, he soon returned to his basket in the hallway but not before dragging his backside across the carpet, an unintentional gesture from the much-loved silky terrier which Henry did not see, and if he had, would have been less than pleased.

"Henry, you mustn't yell obscenities when the children are within hearing range." Freddy wasn't the only ears to prick when Henry shouted. Claire entered Henry's office to counsel him against bad language.

"I'm sorry but I've lost a patient's file and I need it this afternoon."

"I presume you've looked in your desk?"

Henry snapped. "Of course, I have. I'm not stupid."

"Just asking, dear."

Not wishing to aggravate her irascible partner further, Claire promptly left him to clean up his own mess, his boorishness failing to impress. Henry of late had been moody. Not the man she had loved since high school and had three beautiful children with. Was it the pressure of the job or was it something else?

Whatever the reason, Claire was concerned.

Aldgate
Sunday 30 August 1868

The young boy had been in a deep sleep but the door banging loudly followed by raised voices caused him to stir. The voices were rowdy, but not angry. His mother was home with a friend. They were drunk. It wasn't the first time she'd come home in such a state.

Aldrich turned over in his bed. His single mattress was uncomfortable, and rolling during the night was a constant. Uneven and lumpy, he would wake with sore spots. Despite the occasional grumble, his mother told him he'd have to accept his lot in life. He was luckier than most children of his age, she would say, and having a roof over his head gave him an advantage that many other children in the borough could not brag about. The explanation never satisfied but apart from grizzling, he was the child, and his rights were limited.

Despite the bibulous ramblings of his mother and friend in the next room, Aldrich ignored the sounds long enough to fall back to sleep. At least he wasn't home alone. The presence of adults made him feel more protected. His room could be so remote at night.

Scary, sometimes. How long he'd been asleep for he did not know but there was a presence. Who else was in his bed? He was being cuddled, someone pressing up hard against his body. There was a hand on his stomach. And then there was the smell of the alcohol-fouled breath. So putrid.

The other room was now hushed.

Aldrich was quiet, not a muscle moving, and not knowing whether it was his mother in bed with him or a stranger. He wanted to speak but his mouth was dry. Apprehensive, an uneasy feeling was holding him back. This shouldn't be happening.

"Okay luvy ... you 'ave nuffin to worry about."

The words were whispered. Spoken by a female but not his mother. A hand soon moved below his stomach. The touch of the hand was light, gentle. But it wasn't a welcoming hand. Aldrich suppressed the impulse to cry out not knowing what may follow.

Where was his mother? At that moment he needed her. Desperately. She was the only person who could protect him from what was happening. The hand was rubbing his tummy. Still gently. Still lightly. The seconds turned into minutes, the minutes into ...

Aldrich opened his eyes. Light was filtering through the partly draped bedroom window. Dawn had broken. Aldrich rolled over in his bed and found he was alone.

Relief.

He couldn't remember falling back to sleep. Had he been dreaming? No. There was a stranger in his bed. The bad breath, and the unwanted hands that were caressing his body.

He got out of bed, pulled on his trousers that had been flung to the floor with little care the night before and opened the door to the next room. His mother, still fully clothed, was passed out on the couch. There was an empty bottle by her side.

They were alone.

In his eleven short years Aldrich had never felt so relieved.

Chapter 5

Spitalfields

Friday 9 November 1888

The woman was running late. Not unusual because she spent her life being late. Late for friends and late with the rent. It was the hectic life she led. A chaos that she hopefully would soon leave behind.

She had arranged to meet a friend at Ten Bells pub on Commercial Street in the early evening. They liked to have frequent contact but their get togethers of late had been intermittent. The pub was a preference. The people knew her trade, the clientele in the main respectful, providing her with an income when her rent was due. Slim with a fair complexion, patrons invariably described her as rather pleasing to the eye and a real beauty. Her soft Irish brogue also appealed to many of the regulars.

Attracting men was never a problem. And in her line of work that was exceedingly helpful.

On this occasion her friend, Lizzie, was even tardier, arriving thirty minutes after the pre-arranged time. Adding insult, Lizzie could only stay for one drink because she had a second engagement that evening. Lizzie apologised profusely. Undaunted, the woman had also arranged to meet a group of friends at the Horn of Plenty, a pub near where she lived. No need to stress.

Just one of those nights. Both women had other commitments. Another catch up was scheduled for two days' time when they'd have more time to natter. And drink!

After leaving Ten Bells, the woman spent several hours with her friends at the Horn of Plenty on Dorset Street, near to her single room rental. By the time she'd left the pub after midnight, she was unsteady on her feet. Her two female companions were not faring much better. A productive session in terms of drinks imbibed.

Thankfully, the woman didn't have far to go. Only a short walk from the Dorset Street hotel to Millers Court where she lived.

The sparsely furnished, twelve-foot square room had a bed, three tables and a chair. A little used fireplace was in one corner of the room. Above the fireplace hung a print of The Fisherman's Widow. On her less sober nights she would sit with drink in hand, weeping for the woman whose husband was lost at sea. Distraught, the wife in the painting was being comforted by the older woman. The loss was raw.

The woman who rented the room at 13 Miller's Court could empathise.

She had travelled that road herself. Married at sixteen, her husband died in a coal mining accident three years later. Understanding the many dangers of the mining industry, she'd pleaded with him to find other work, but her pleas had fallen on deaf ears. When the news came through of the accident, she wasn't surprised.

But grief stricken she was. Though young at the time, she'd found love and when that love was taken from her so cruelly it left a big hole in her heart. A hole that had yet to fully heal.

Her affection for her husband extended to the female friends in her life who also did tricks to earn a living. On the worst of the wintry nights, she would invite them to stay in her room. Not the most lavish of establishments, but they were safe from the bleakest of the elements. Discovered by her landlord who disapproved of her kindness, she was repeatedly warned to stop bringing in guests. Or else!

He was such a bloody bugger. It wasn't as if the extra bodies in her room affected him. He still got his damn money.

As she entered her room, the rent she owed played on her mind. Some twenty-nine shillings in arrears. A large sum. She'd have to work long hours and fulfill the cravings of many-a-client the next day. Fortunately, it was a Saturday so there'd be plenty of men looking for a good time. She should've been out and about earning a few shillings that night, but drinking with old friends was more enticing.

The woman was also keen to return to Limerick. She'd had enough of London and the sordid toil that kept her alive. There had to be more to life than complying with men's sexual deviances and listening to their never-ending grievances and tales of misfortune.

She understood misfortune, but these men were just sooks.

Kicking off her shoes but without undressing, her body wilting after a night of drinking, the woman fell onto the bed, exhausted. Lying on her back, her eyes soon closed. She didn't hear the door open and the creaking floorboards. The pain was intense as the blade was thrust deep into her neck. But there was no murmur from the victim, the liquor blunting her senses.

Soon her eyes would be shut, permanently.

The stranger took his time, confident he would not be disturbed. He enjoyed his work. Starting with the abdomen and thighs, the knife was driven into the body, ruthlessly.

Next, the woman's breasts were targeted. It only took seconds to cut through the soft tissue. One breast was deposited under the head, the other breast by the right foot. Her face was cut. Viciously. The face the clients so fancied. The Irish rose. Chopped. Only frightful gashes remained. Parts of her nose, cheeks, eyebrows, and ears were removed.

The stranger was almost done.

Her liver was placed at her feet; the intestines by the right side of the body; the spleen by the left side. On one of the tables and under the print of The Fisherman's Widow, the folds from the woman's abdomen and thighs were callously discarded.

Satisfied, the stranger, cane in hand, left. He had been in the woman's room for over an hour. Longer than expected.

The next morning the landlord's assistant came for the woman's rent. After knocking once and not getting a response, he looked through the keyhole, but couldn't see anyone moving about. Access to the room could also be made through two windows that opened up to a side yard. A broken windowpane had been stuffed with clothes to keep out the wind, so he pulled the clothing away.

Peering inside for a second time the bloody scene shocked.

Spread out on the bed, her dignity stripped to the core, the woman's body was mutilated beyond recognition. Her face was slashed, and her heart was missing.

The walls were showered with her blood. The floor and bed were also blood spattered. Hardly a square foot of the room didn't contain the blood of the twenty-five-year-old. The horribly disfigured body had a permanent impact on the hardened officers who attended the crime scene. What they saw would stay with them. Forever. Such was the atrocious condition of the corpse, identification was only possible through recognition of her ear and her blue eyes. Even her gender was hard to distinguish.

Police deduced burnt fabrics in the fireplace grate were the woman's clothes, providing the light for the mutilation to occur. The only other light found in the room was a single candle placed on top of a chipped wine glass.

What was not considered at the time by the police and her friends was that a scream could have been enough to save the woman. The building housed other tenants and a neighbour may have heard her cries, if indeed there was a cry for help. The alcohol she'd consumed made the killer's job so much easier.

Months later as the authorities continued to investigate the so-called Ripper murders, the general conclusion was that Mary-Jane was Jack the Ripper's last victim. There had been no further murders since the Irish woman's demise. The crime spree ended because of the perpetrator's death, imprisonment, institutionalisation, or emigration to one of the colonies. That was the official line to the press, but no one really knew. It was pure guesswork on the part of the constabulary.

A fearful public was not convinced and was demanding answers.

Walking along the cobblestone road, the man was barefoot. It was tough going because of the uneven nature of the bricks underfoot. His feet were sore and slightly bloodied, but he kept up the pace despite his toes trapping the occasional stone.

It was dusk and the lamplighters, lugging long ladders, were attending to the gas lamps. A job they did early morning and early evening every day of the year. The gas lamps were sparsely placed along the road. The life of a lamplighter, the man decided, was laborious. A thankless job. But a job was a job.

He had no idea where he was walking to or who he was supposed to meet. But on he walked. As he approached a fork in the road, he looked down, but no longer could he see his toes. Black boots were now covering his broken skin. Stopping outside a shop, his reflection in the window revealed his attire: a black felt hat and a long cane.

The transformation dazzled.

He was a gentleman of means, he thought admiringly. Not like the riff raff and the uncouth who existed in this part of London.

The man was mightily pleased with himself. Continuing his walk, he was aware of two women approaching at speed. They soon crossed onto his side of the road. They were headed for him. The nature of their caper soon became apparent. Their overdone blush cheeks and bright red lips told the story. Both were curvaceous but not fat, plentiful bosom exposed. Showing no interest, the man extended his stride.

"... 'Ang on luv," said one woman. "Just wanna chat."

"Why is you in such an 'urry?" the other woman said, inhaling deeply between strides.

The fury was building within, but he refused to speak. These filthy vermin had one thing in mind, and he wouldn't be part of their fraudulent livelihoods. There was no acknowledgement of either woman as he upped his pace. He wasn't about to be distracted by these no-hopers.

"Come on. You ... a man of such rank ... you'd like to 'ave fun. Yvie and me friend Mabel 'ere would be 'appy to take part in whatever ... 'at right Mabel?"

The first woman was not going to be ignored by this toff. Because they had money and privilege, they thought they were better than them. Bugger that! Just born lucky, many inheriting their fortunes. Hard work. Huh! Wouldn't know what hard work was. Fuck the lot of them.

The man stopped suddenly, the women almost hurtling into him. Raising his cane, he struck the first woman hard across the head. She squealed in pain. The second woman was quicker to act and raised a defensive arm knocking the cane as it brushed her stomach.

The man's combative act was accompanied by a string of foul words, the women calling him every name under the sun. He wasn't listening. He didn't care.

Taking flight, a further fifty feet on, the man crossed the road, confident the women would no longer be a bother.

Rounding a corner and deciding he was safe from harassment, he paused at another shop window to admire his apparel. The black hat, the long, dark coat with a fur-trimmed collar and the cane. A picture of sartorial elegance. Such grace. Such refinement. How he came into money he couldn't recall but money he definitely had. Twice twirling his moustache, he walked off.

Soon after he saw the woman leave the Horn of Plenty, a drab establishment he would not be seen dead in. Another vulgar and unkempt local, the man decided, who'd probably had a skinful. He followed at a distant so as not to be seen. She was staggering which was no big surprise. Most of these types drank too much ... as well as selling their bodies.

Little morality in these parts. They behaved worse than alley cats.

The woman entered 13 Miller's Court through a side alleyway, the man ten feet behind. She opened a door to an apartment and went inside. The man waited a few minutes. Turning the handle, the door was unlocked. He could make out the woman on the bed. Licking his lips, he closed the door and got out a knife.

Slash after slash. Intestine and other body bits flew across the bed and onto the floor. There was no stopping now. He had whipped himself into a delirium. Blood was pouring from the deep wounds but on he went. The blows to the woman's body became more frenzied. A euphoria he'd experienced before and couldn't get enough of. "The bitch must die!"

"The bitch must die!" Henry shouted the words.

The routine was all too familiar. Claire switched on the bedside lamp. Another Henry nightmare. Dear god, when would it end?

"The woman had everything cut off. There was so much blood," said Henry, agitated and catching his breath.

"It's okay. It was just a dream, Henry. Please, calm, you'll wake the kids." Claire's pacifying words failed to sway Henry.

"No. I was there. I killed that woman. I remember it clearly now. Stalking her; following her home; creeping into her room and cutting her. Tearing at her flesh. I kept plunging the knife into her body. Claire it was dreadful. I couldn't stop. I didn't want to stop."

Henry began to weep.

Claire placed a caring arm around Henry. Sobbing like a baby, both he and Claire didn't move from their bed for an hour. When he had finally stopped whimpering, he addressed his dozing partner. Calmly.

"Claire, this may sound weird, but I think I know what's happening. The dreams. The murdered women. I've seen how each one of the victims died. How would I know unless I was there ... an onlooker, a witness."

Claire was about to speak but was silenced by Henry's tormented eyes.

"Hear me out. Only one explanation. I committed these despicable crimes. I mutilated these women. I'm Jack the Ripper!"

"Jack the Ripper!" Aghast, Claire burst into tears. "Nonsense, Henry. What are you saying? These are just dreams, but you need help." Claire was living her own nightmare. Henry, her childhood sweetheart, confidant and lover was losing his mind.

The sandstone building had stood for over 125 years, along with many other buildings on this side of the city. Henry gazed up at each of the five levels, or at least pretended to, as office workers passed him by oblivious to his meanderings. The brickwork had worn well. There were no visible chips or cracks. Sandstone was durable and many of the city's buildings were made of the stone. But it wasn't the only reason he stood there in the early morning sunshine.

Henry was procrastinating, badly. For the moment, he kept peering upwards.

He had arranged to meet an old friend. They went through medical school together and while Henry was into his thirteenth year as a general practitioner, his mate had furthered his studies and become a psychiatrist, having had an interest in the brain and mental health.

While happy to see an old friend, Henry wasn't thrilled about divulging the actual reason he'd come to see him. Telling Claire he would see someone about the nightmares, he was on a promise, but the catch up had been made under some duress. For days he'd ummed and erred about seeing his friend before making the phone call.

It wasn't an official appointment, as such, more of a casual meeting between old friends. That was it. An informal get together. Henry was happy with that train of thought.

After spending five minutes on the pavement, Henry got up enough courage to walk through the double doors into the foyer. While there'd been past visits, he had to check the screen at ground level to confirm where his old friend worked. His mind was not focussed but the information was soon forthcoming. Doctor Michael Jenkins Level 4. Henry took the lift and at reception was greeted by a young girl with ponytails and buck teeth.

"I'm here to see Michael. He knows I'm coming," said a fidgety Henry.

"And your name?" The girl smiled as she picked up the phone.

"Henry Evans."

Henry was directed to an adjoining room where six chairs were neatly arranged around a table piled high with magazines. What doctor's rooms didn't have myriad journals, usually of the kitschy celebrity type? Flicking through one of the magazines, occasionally he would peer out the large glass windows onto North Terrace. Located in the heart of Adelaide and home to some of the city's oldest architecture dating back to its 19th century settlement, the terrace was a thoroughfare for cars and trams. The nearby hills were just to the east and the beachside suburbs were further to the west.

Many prominent institutions including the museum, the art gallery and parliament could be found on the wide, tree-lined terrace. The wine centre, a favourite of Henry's, was also within walking distance.

Henry couldn't count the number of times the family had visited the museum; the dinosaur display was one of John's great joys. A recent exhibition featuring a replica of the largest Tyrannosaurus rex ever found captivated John for hours. Claire, Harriet and Lucy had little interest in dinosaurs and strolled around the other displays. A reluctant volunteer, Henry stayed with his son while he inspected every dinosaur bone. And there were hundreds of bones!

The beast known as Scotty was almost thirteen metres long. John walked back and forth from head to tail ... and back again. He was in awe. There wasn't a section of the dinosaur that he hadn't studied. Seeing the giant head and the long teeth, John was goggle-eyed. While Henry appreciated his young son's fascination with the extinct Scotty, spending so much time with 66-million-year-old bones was beyond boring. Henry's belief was that once you were dead you were dead, and the bones should stay buried. Then again, he was a doctor and not a palaeontologist.

Leaving thoughts of dinosaurs behind and about to pick up another trashy magazine, a face appeared through the open door. Henry offered his hand.

"Henry, good to see you."

"You to, Michael."

"I've only got about fifteen minutes until my next appointment. Sorry, but life in the fast lane ... as you would appreciate."

Michael Jenkins was taller than Henry and built like a rugby player. Henry often thought that if anyone was mad enough to confront Michael in a dark alley, they'd come off second best. The broad shoulders and the large hands. No contest. Unlike Henry, he had a full head of dark hair and a thick, wavy moustache. One of the more jovial types at medical school, Henry always enjoyed his company, but family and work life had prevented more frequent get-togethers.

"I gather this isn't just a social visit. Without giving much away you sounded a tad sullen on the phone last week."

"That's a fair assessment." Henry was never comfortable talking about his own problems, especially with a colleague. Not that he believed himself invincible, but he was the doctor, and it was his job to help others. That's why he got into medicine in the first place. "Not sure how to begin. It all sounds a little weird."

"As they say in the classics, let's start at the beginning." Michael Jenkins was more than a little intrigued by his friend's reluctance to open up. Probing Henry closely, he could sense the discomfort.

"Yes. Sitting here with my mouth closed won't achieve much. As I said it's going to sound weird, but

I've been having these visions, nightmares ... not just any nightmare but a recurring nightmare."

Pausing, Henry hadn't felt so awkward since his high school days.

"Go on, Henry."

"I've done research and I think I've been witnessing the Ripper murders in London. I've seen the women being hacked to death, butchered. I've woken up in a real state let me tell you. I keep waking Claire. It's not fair on her. Without sounding ridiculous, it's been a bloody nightmare ... and I'm not trying to be funny." The account of recent events spilled from his mouth, Henry almost tripping over the words.

The room was hushed, then Michael Jenkins spoke. "Have you been pushing it too hard at work? What about home? Are you and Claire, okay? The kids?"

"Fair questions. The practice is busy, but I've been working long hours for years. Nothing has really changed. As for me and Claire. All good on that front. The children are fine so no worries there either."

"I presume you don't have a history of bad dreams."

"Totally out of the blue. I have no idea why things have suddenly changed. Fucking unbelievable! I even dreamt that poor Freddy was slaughtered; bits of him all over the side of the house."

"Freddy?"

"The family dog." In a few short minutes, Henry was worn-out from explaining his recent health issues and wondered what his friend would make of it. If anyone had told Henry such a story, he would've called for them to be institutionalised and locked up for good.

"Strange it is," said Michael Jenkins thoughtfully, but without a trace of a smile. "It's hard to say Henry, but I would start by reducing your work hours and see if that helps. You wouldn't believe how many patients I've seen who've tipped over the edge from working too hard. Burnt out at a relatively young age. The will to succeed and to be the best. To be better than everyone else. And on it goes."

"You sound like Claire. She's been telling me that for ages."

"Claire always struck me as the sensible one in your family. If you would like a formal appointment, I could recommend a good friend of mine. I'm not quite comfortable seeing you in an official capacity. The ethical thing as we are friends if you get my drift."

"I understand, Michael. I've fulfilled a promise to Claire to have a chat, but I don't think I need to be psychoanalysed to the nth degree, and I don't mean that rudely."

"No offense taken but if you change your mind, you have my number."

"Thanks, old mate, sure do."

Henry left the building feeling guilty that he'd short-changed his friend by not disclosing everything. He held back on his belief that in a past life he was Jack the Ripper. But if he'd come out with that pearler his friend may have gone into a tailspin.

Some things are not easily told to friends and relatives.

The thought of being surrounded by people in long, white coats and prescribed heavy meds was not his idea of fun. Henry wasn't willing to accept that outcome. Not at any cost. For the time being, he and Claire would keep the nightmares close to their chests. Henry had come from a long line of doctors starting with his great-great-grandfather.

He had a tradition to uphold. His reputation could be in serious trouble if anyone learnt of his Ripper theory.

Chapter 6
Aldgate
Sunday 24 June 1888

Bertha Eckersley would have been happy with small talk. Any reaction from her husband to placate her growing disquiet. A grunt or two. A belch. Even flatulence. Any sound would be welcome. Aldrich had been sullen for weeks. He got up early for work and came home late from work. He ate his dinner, silently, then read for an hour or two and retired for the night. Monday to Saturday the routine did not vary. Aldrich was of the type who gave little away.

Sundays were the exception. A variation to the daily humdrum: a stroll around the local borough to break the monotony. Good heavens, on occasions they even walked arm in arm and the odd word would escape from his mouth.

While Bertha welcomed the Sunday outings, she couldn't fathom why they always traced the same route. Aldrich was a creature of habit, and for unknown reasons the impoverished areas fascinated. He delighted in seeing how the other half lived. The down and outs. Or so it seemed. Querying why the same well-trodden path was taken each Sunday, Bertha once received a disapproving grunt and an indignant eye. An eye that only Aldrich could give.

The question was not raised again.

Never commenting about what he observed, it was the silence that unsettled Bertha. Passing judgement on these poor unfortunates. Bertha sensed her husband had condemned them as a burden on society, making unfair assumptions and writing them off as worthless.

Wondering at times why she'd married Aldrich, on his best days she'd admit there were upsides. The marriage wasn't all bad. A handy tradesman, he brought in a reasonable salary as a stonemason while her meagre take home pay as a seamstress at a local haberdashery topped up the family income. The combined earnings meant they had a reasonable standard of living.

The three small rooms they rented above a shoe shop in Fenchurch Street more than catered for their trifling needs. Apart from the occasional couple they greeted on their Sunday strolls they hardly ever fraternised.

Walks around the nearby slums was evidence enough that life was far tougher for many others. The tiny, grimy faces and the tatty, torn clothes: children playing in and amongst the waste in the smelly, diseased streets. Penniless.

Heart-breaking. The pitiful sights made Bertha tear up.

Bertha assumed Aldrich was displeased with his work situation but there was a stubborn refusal for any discussion. While Aldrich spent twelve-hour days, six days a week at work, Bertha's days were not as long, and she was often home by five o'clock to prepare the evening meal. They usually ate two hours later. The meals were not grandiose but there was always sufficient on the table. Neither drank alcohol as Aldrich refused to have liquor on the premises.

Aldrich had his good points. For one he never complained about Bertha's cooking. This was part of the marriage that made her the happiest. Her mother, along with teaching her the finer points of cursive, passed on simple cooking skills that in married life had proved expedient. She would never pick up a chef's position at a tavern in Leicester Square or Piccadilly, but the meals were wholesome and tasty.

Aldrich's knack of walking between rooms without being heard was unsettling, but Bertha had learnt to live with his strange, unpredictable ways. Separate bedrooms suited because Bertha slept deeply while her husband was a light sleeper and tended to toss and turn. It was a mutual decision agreed to early in their marriage to have separate beds. The arrangement worked. Sex didn't play a big part in their relationship and whenever Aldrich felt the urge he'd tap twice on Bertha's door. Mercifully, Aldrich wasn't in the mood that often and when he was Bertha never denied him.

Without complaint she would quench his sexual appetite as wives had a duty to satisfy their husband's needs. Her mother used to say that men's eyes would only wander if they were not looked after in the home. Bertha never quite accepted that argument, but she carried out her wifely duties the best she could.

The only time Aldrich shocked was early in their marriage when Bertha was preparing supper. Without as much as a word Aldrich approached, lifted her dress, tore at her corset and had his way with her from behind. Roughly. The action was so swift and unexpected, Bertha had little time to protest. The thrusting was not pleasant but denying her husband was hardly the done thing. She knew not what to say. Such erratic behaviour had not occurred since, so Bertha had no reason to talk to Aldrich about what had happened. She pushed the incident to the back of her mind. There it would stay.

Aldrich's strange habits could manifest at any time of the day. There were nights when Bertha thought she'd heard the front door open, but Aldrich vehemently denied he had left the building.

Goodness gracious. Never. He told Bertha nightly walks were not for him. Too many dangerous types roaming around the seedy laneways and backstreets of Aldgate. He had pronounced loudly and more than once to Bertha that only a fool would walk the streets at night.

And as Bertha often did, she took her husband at his word.

Henry knew Claire would demand a full account of his meeting with Michael Jenkins, even though he was just seeing an old friend. Catch up or appointment? It was splitting hairs. The finer details to him were less important. The fact was he had kept an undertaking to his partner. The promise was one thing, but Henry was secretly concerned about his mental state and the nightmares.

The truth could be more frightening than the dreams. What was triggering them? Was it simply a case of over work? If so, he'd have to give serious thought to reducing his hours, at least until he was better.

Claire heard Henry come in the front door. He was home earlier than usual. They hadn't had a chance to chat during the day, but she was desperate to hear how his appointment went. Problems with the children came and went, as they did with all families, but Henry believing that he was Jack the Ripper was top of the charts. There wasn't an hour of each day where she hadn't thought about what he'd said that night. The disclosure. The disbelief. It was the number one thing on her mind.

Jack the Ripper! He had to be joking!

Henry had always been fairly mild-mannered and was incapable of hurting anyone. That's why he became a doctor. To help people. Even if Claire believed in reincarnation or people who'd lived a past life, and she didn't, that did not mean he was a monster or that any part of that reprehensible human being had or would show up in Henry. Not in the 21st century. Not in Henry the man she loved; her childhood sweetheart; the father of her three children.

Jack the Ripper. How preposterous! Totally over the top.

Claire laughed at her own silliness. The rice was almost ready, but she continued to stir the pot as Henry entered the kitchen. Anticipating Henry's question, Claire said, "The children are upstairs doing their homework ... well, Harriet and Lucy are. John is watching television, so we are alone. For now. So how did it go?" Claire said, making sure she got in first.

"You don't waste any time." Henry's lips brushed Claire's cheek.

"I'm worried about you so no, I'm not wasting time, Henry."

"Michael said to say hi by the way, and I'm not procrastinating." Almost laughing, Henry knew full well that he was stalling, but he first had to get the preliminaries out of the way.

"That's nice. So!"

"I told him about the dreams, and he said I'm probably over worked. Need to slow down."

Claire let out a mighty whoop. "Yes, go Michael. What else? He must have said more than that." Henry wasn't going to get off the hook that easily.

"Well, in all honesty ... not really. I only had fifteen minutes with him until his next appointment, so it wasn't a long talk."

"Bloody hell, Henry! You've had me worried sick for weeks. You told me you're Jack the Ripper. You need help."

"No, what I said was I believed I was Jack the Ripper in a past life. Big difference, Claire."

"It's still bloody crazy stuff. Listen to what you're saying." Claire stirred the rice with more vigour, her temperament replicating the bubbling pot on the stove.

"I haven't had a nightmare for a while now. This thing could be over. Done and dusted."

Claire stopped stirring the pot, turned down the heat, and sat with Henry at the table. "Sweetheart, I've been terribly worried about your state of mind. Not everyone tells their partner they're Jack the Ripper. Call me silly. Call me overprotective. But it's not an every-day thing."

"I know how it sounds, Claire."

"No, you don't. You need to take care of yourself, and you need to see Michael or someone else if you like. These dreams may be over, and we may never know what caused them but ... they may not go away. For god's sake, you're not Jack the Ripper. Get that stu-pid thought out of your head once and for all."

Henry carefully considered Claire's words. They were coming from the heart. "Okay. I'll call Michael tomorrow. He doesn't want me as a client because of professional ethics, but he has a friend who he can rec-ommend. I trust him."

"Thanks darling." Claire gave Henry an appreciative kiss when John, dressed in a Batman suit, ran into the kitchen waving his arms.

"Dinner. I'm starved! I've been catching bad guys."

Henry and Claire laughed.

"Why are you laughing?" John was serious about being hungry. Catching crooks on the other hand was make believe. Still, he didn't like his parents laughing at him.

"Sorry, darling," said Claire. "You look adorable in your Batman suit. Not laughing at you but with you."

John smiled. Mummy's words seemed reasonable. Not that he fully understood the difference.

Henry and Claire knew their talk about another ap-pointment would have to wait. And further talk of Jack the Ripper would have to take a back seat to a hungry six-year-old. The little things in life. The cherished things in life.

Priceless!

Blowing strongly earlier in the evening, the wind by midnight had moderated to the odd gust. Drowsy and not fully awake, Henry rolled over in bed, mindful the weather had calmed.

His eyes opened. There was a noise from downstairs. It could've been Freddy scratching. The vagaries of the weather could affect Freddy as well. Dogs were no different to people, especially Freddy who was regarded as a dear family member. Teachers often complained that students were rattier on a windy day, and Henry believed Freddy suffered from the same disorder.

Henry lay for a few more minutes before going downstairs. He didn't want to investigate as the events of the past few months had made him slightly paranoid. Descending the stairs, the hallway light was dimmed, but he soon saw Freddy, his two back legs were rigid and protruding from his basket.

An earthquake wouldn't shake Freddy awake.

Henry made his way to the kitchen when his attention was drawn to another noise. Upstairs this time. A person was whimpering. In the top drawer next to the sink was a carving knife. Knives had played a distressing part in Henry's dreams, and he considered boycotting the drawer. But only momentarily.

Soon the knife was in his hand.

Had someone broken into the house? Were the kids in danger?

Henry climbed the stairs. Hovering outside Harriet's bedroom, he cocked his ears. The dying wind was barely audible now. About to enter his daughter's bedroom, the whining noise was heard again. It wasn't coming from Harriet's room but from further down the hallway.

Standing outside Lucy's bedroom the disturbance was clearer. The moaning was that of an older person, not a child. Henry raised the knife, uneasily, as he turned the handle, fearing that his daughter was in danger. No time to dilly-dally.

There may be no second chances.

Pushing the door open, the knife firmly in hand, Henry stepped into Lucy's bedroom. Startled by the shadow and the hand on his arm, Henry struck out with the knife. Not once but twice. In the dark the body slumped to the ground. Henry searched for the bedroom light, his hand slapping the wall. Frantically.

The light flickered on ....

Her pyjama top was turning red, blood pouring from a deep wound to her stomach. The life in her young body was quickly ebbing.

"Fuck. What've I done?"

His little girl was dying. As he knelt down cradling Lucy, Henry, his body shaking violently, screamed for help.

Claire's help.

Sitting on the sofa the children were restless. Claire and Henry were standing. Only one minute into the family meeting and the moans and groans had begun. Believing it was a moment of some importance, Freddy joined the family, curling up on the floor, his snout resting on John's sandal. Harriet was keen for a quick meeting as she had a netball game at ten that morning. It was fast approaching nine o'clock. One win away from a grand final appearance, the game's significance was colossal. A loss and the season was over. Henley Beach, also known as the Henley Hawks, would be out of the competition.

Claire spoke first.

"Dad and I need to talk to you before we go our separate ways with Saturday sports. This is important. We won't make you late for your game, Harrie ... I promise."

Harriet grumbled loudly. When mum and dad dropped the t in her name, they were either being pleasant or after something. On this occasion, she suspected, it was the latter. Being the eldest, Harriet knew that if she was accepting, Lucy and John would fall into place and follow her lead. So, what scheme were her parents hatching? It could be a doozy. Harriet could hardly wait to hear what they'd cooked up.

Continuing, Claire said, "You may have heard dad scream last night. Believe me, it would've been heard two suburbs away. So loud. I almost died a thousand deaths." Claire smiled but her witticism did not get a response, the children wondering where this was all leading.

"Mum, I didn't hear a thing." This family chat was so unnecessary. Harriet's patience was wearing thin. Now ticking past nine, she wanted to leave. She hated being late. None of her teammates would be late. And it was the preliminary final. What did her parents not get? Honestly!

"Calm down Harriet, I won't be long. Dad has been having nightmares and we don't know what's causing them. He's been to see a specialist and he plans to see him again soon."

"We just want to make sure you guys are okay," said Henry, deciding it was time to add his two cents worth. Only fair, considering he was the cause of the family drama.

"Why wouldn't we be okay," said Harriet, her voice raised. "This is so silly."

Claire remained calm despite her daughter's bellicosity. "As I said, dad yelled out in his sleep last night and we want to make sure no one was frightened by what occurred."

Without warning, Lucy laughed. Henry and Claire traded a surprised glance.

"What's so funny, dear?" said Claire.

"Dad's been talking in his sleep for ever. In between his snoring. He says the funniest things." Lucy giggled again while Harriet and John were struggling to see what was so hilarious.

"So, you've heard me before?"

"Thousands of times, daddy ... you're funny."

"I'm glad you find me funny."

"And you've never been concerned? Claire asked, puzzled by her daughter's reaction.

Lucy paused. "Well, I had a bad dream last night. Daddy tried to hurt me, but it was only a dream."

Henry and Claire were appalled.

"What was the dream about, sweetie?" said Henry.

"You were bad, that's all. But I love you, Daddy."

"Love you too." Henry was ready to cry. He would cut off an arm or a leg before physically harming any of his children.

Claire and Henry were unsure what to say next. They were disturbed that Lucy had had a nightmare. Lucy was the most chilled of the children, but their ten-year-old's admission still stunned. Did she see a knife in her dream? What other ghastly thing did she dream about?

"I've had other bad dreams," Lucy added.

"Really ..." Henry could barely speak.

"Please tell us in future, darling," said Claire. "We only want to help,"

Lucy shrugged. "Okay."

Standing, Harriet said, "Seriously. We've all had bad dreams. I'm off. Come on, Dad." Finding the discussion tiresome and with her anxiety rising about being late, Harriet headed for the front door, leaving Lucy and John who were clueless as to what had taken place. Freddy saw an opening and leapt onto the sofa and soon occupied Harriet's spot.

Henry and Claire, unlike the children, were not so cheery. Henry had taken ages to settle after waking at the foot of the bed screaming his lungs out. Believing he'd knifed Lucy, it was the most shocking of all his dreams. Like the other nightmares it seemed genuine.

Claire was white with shock after experiencing another of Henry's night terrors and her nerves were starting to fray. Both trembling, they had held one another until first light. Despite their troubled night, they had to ensure the children were not being affected by the bizarre happenings.

"I better go. Harriet will throw a tantrum if I don't get her to netball on time." Henry went to the kitchen and got the car keys from the table. He left the house still reeling from Lucy's shock admission that she'd been hurt by him in a dream.

Claire on the other hand was floored by Lucy's blasé reaction. That she appeared unmoved by the nightmares was pleasing but odd. "Okay you two, what are you up to this morning?"

"Cartoons," said John, racing for the TV remote, remembering it was Saturday morning.

"I'll do some drawing in my room, Mum." Lucy skipped from the room.

The discussion had not gone the way she and Henry had envisaged. Not at all. Lucy had had a nightmare, like her father. A nightmare that didn't seem to worry her unduly. John was none-the-wiser, and their teenage daughter only had sport on her mind. And because she was of that age, soon to be boys.

That age! Goodness.

Claire remembered the difficult time she gave her parents as a teenager. If Harriet was half as bad, then they were in for a torrid few years.

Another thing to add to her list of worries.

For the moment at least she was off the parental hook for home errands and child-minding. Harriet was on her way to netball; John was in front of the television and Lucy was drawing in her room. Peace in our time. Claire headed to the kitchen to make a cup of tea. Boy, did she need one!

These night terrors were damaging. Claire was convinced Henry had to talk to Michael Jenkins again. And the sooner, the better.

Chapter 7
Aldgate
Sunday 30 September 1868

Aldrich lay awake in bed.

He didn't know the time, but it was late. His mother would come in the door soon, probably drunk again. She rarely came home sober. If Aldrich had luck on his side his mother would be alone and not with a friend tagging along. The woman in his bed had frightened him, terribly. Still unsure why she cuddled him and touched him where she shouldn't have, Aldrich was determined to be alert, even if it meant staying awake all night. His choices were few because the bedroom door had no lock, and he couldn't block the entrance with furniture. Apart from the bed, there was little else in his room.

The banging door woke him. He'd fallen asleep despite his best efforts to stay awake. His mother could be heard in the other room. She was slurring. Talking to someone. The other woman was also slurring, so the exact nature of the conversation was lost on Aldrich. Through the closed door they were hard to hear. Except for the occasional word or two.

"Lovely, he was ... She's a bitch. Someone will do her in."

Aldrich's body tensed. Involuntarily. This is not what he wanted. What if it was the same person? She'd come to his bed like the last time and do things to him. His damp leg. The moist mattress. His mother would be so upset that he'd wet his bed. He'd have to clean the mattress in the morning. How could he be so stupid? Last time it happened he was yelled at badly. There was also a hard slap across the face.

A night spent lying on a wet mattress. Hell no! Aldrich started to sob. That his mother would have strangers in his home that hurt him was cruel. He hated his life and he hated where he lived.

Above all, he hated his mother.

Aldgate
Monday 1 October 1888

As soon as Aldrich had left the house for work, Bertha went to her desk and opened her journal. She always found it easier to write when her husband was at work. Even though Aldrich had denied, many times, that he never went out at night, Bertha was now convinced he wasn't being truthful. The front door of their first-floor residence had definitely opened at an early hour. The exact time was unknown, but it must've been after midnight. She hadn't retired until eleven o'clock which was unusually late for her. She'd nodded off for a time and presumed it was early morning when the creaking door woke her.

Tempted to check on Aldrich, she resisted. Not a great sleeper, if he was in bed awake a check on his well-being would only make him cranky. Another of his idiosyncrasies. He was very guarded at times, so it was an outcome Bertha had to avoid.

The latest entry, Bertha decided, had to be more of a realistic appraisal of the current standing of their relationship. After all, what were journals for other than to disclose a person's most intimate feelings. With pen in hand, Bertha, as was her standard writing method, meticulously formed the thoughts and sentences in her head before committing the words to paper.

'Sunday included our usual morning stroll. While Aldrich took my arm in his, he seemed even more distant. Few words did he say. His thoughts remained his thoughts. No one we knew passed us in the street and our stroll lasted less than an hour. Upon our return home, Aldrich read the newspaper and I busied myself cleaning the house and preparing the nightly meal. A pleasant enough day if one is being honest with oneself. Where Aldrich and I are in terms of our marriage I cannot say. He never speaks disapprovingly of me and what I do. Then again, he never says much at all. He's become moodier as the weeks have gone by and I have little understanding as to the reasons why. As my mother often said, God bless her, marriage is not a bed of roses. When a couple commit to marriage, they will endure trials and tribulations. Nothing in God's universe is surer. While I can't say that I am dreadfully displeased, I do feel my life could be cheerier. A little less wearisome. I forever hope and pray that things will turn around for the better. I also pray that Aldrich will want to have children one day. A child's joyful face may be the blessing our family home needs to forsake the dreariness of our lives.'

Bertha put the pen down and closed the journal. Enough said for now. The new week had got off to a mediocre start. But six days were left in the week for the situation to improve.

It'd been a long morning. A terribly long morning for Henry. First, the crisis meeting in the loungeroom to explain his bad dreams to the children. Then came Harriet's netball loss. What began with a confident daughter and her teammates chasing a grand final spot in their division ended in calamity. While Henry had maintained the girls had played brilliantly and a one-goal loss was hardly a failure, nothing could mollify his daughter's devastation.

The Henley Hawks had blown it. The Glenelg Gazelles were through to the grand final.

Perhaps it was the age. A thirteen-year-old in the early stages of puberty. Many things as a teenager seemed like world-ending events. Henry had suffered disappointments in life as everyone does, but he couldn't remember being as disconsolate as his daughter. Not ever.

For the drive home Harriet had demoted herself to the back seat, even though her father had begged her to sit up front with him. The back seat provided sanctuary for her distress. Harriet was determined to be alone. She sobbed all the way home. Not soft snuffles but loud blubbering.

Little of what her father said could console her; his efforts to raise her spirits were futile. Talk of playing brilliantly and an honourable loss fell on deaf ears. Their hearts were set on being in the grand final and they'd fallen short. One goal or twenty. A loss was a bloody loss. This would plague her for years. How could she have botched the game, so miserably? In between the tears, Harriet replayed in her head the final devastating minutes of the match.

Over and over. The result was always the same. Defeat!

The teams had been level pegging for five minutes with easy opportunities missed by both sides. Put down to finals' pressure. Harriet's opponent who was playing goal attack, out manoeuvred her in the final seconds, throwing the ball to the goal shooter up forward who found the net. Harriet should've been on her, toe-to-toe, to thwart any last-minute chances. Allow her no breathing space. But the girl feigned a move forward as she called for the ball, only to quickly drop back, the ball whizzing over Harriet's head. She had been duped and the mistake would remain with her for the rest of her life.

Now the Henley Hawks would have to wait a year to have another crack at a premiership. Sport could be cruel.

Harriet was out of the car as soon as it pulled into the driveway and had bolted inside before the key was out of the ignition, Henry left wondering what other knocks the rest of the day might yield. He went to the kitchen and got a cold beer from the fridge. Longing for a few minutes of solitude, the morning had been trying. Not a brilliant start to the weekend. Henry downed the contents of the can in quick time before reaching for another beer.

Henry and Claire weren't sure how the children would take the news, but after a lengthy discussion believed their proposal would be in everyone's best interest. A week had passed since the family meeting. A gathering that had not been entirely to Henry and Claire's satisfaction. Harriet was filthy about her net-ball loss and on a downhill slide emotionally, and Lucy's admission about having bad dreams and taking it all in her stride was troubling. Then there was Henry's questionable mental health. Doubts remained in Henry's mind about whether he was or wasn't Jack the Ripper. Claire had no such doubts, but his state of mind was cause for concern. Henry's night terrors were also causing her to have restless nights.

The verdict: the family had to get away. A circuit breaker to get them through to Christmas and the school holidays. Claire had made special Sunday morning pancakes. Freddy was on constant sentry under the kitchen table for any errant crumbs that may fall his way. While told it was impolite to talk and eat at the same time, the children were slow to learn the often-recited mantra by their parents. And that was:

Children who talk and eat at the same time equates to food on floor gobbled by greedy dog.

Young John was guilty of dropping pancake bits here, there and everywhere. May not have been deliberate but when John ate, not all the pancake ended in his mouth. Freddy was often spotted at John's feet, realising from his puppy days that the youngest in the family was a sure bet when it came to providing leftovers.

With a generous spread of butter, the toppings of choice were honey, jam and syrup. Claire thought she'd wait until the children had had their fill before mentioning the main reason for pancakes for breakfast. "Anyone for another pancake," she asked, eying the children's almost clean plates.

There were a few nonchalant shakes of the head.

"I'm done," said Lucy.

"No mummy. They were delicious," said John, patting his tummy, and with half a pancake still on his plate. Like a surfacing submarine Freddy's head emerged from under the table.

"Good, glad you liked them, John. Now dad and I want to run something past you."

Harriet rolled her eyes while Lucy munched the last of her pancake, syrup smudging her lips and chin.

"It's important guys," Henry said, noting Harriet's tepid reaction. "And we think you'll like what we're going to say."

The last statement from her father was too much for Harriet who piped up, "No more bad dreams, Dad?"

"No, Harriet." Henry didn't bite, as he did not want to be sucked in by her sarcasm.

"Dad and I are taking you on a holiday ... leaving this afternoon. Camping near Wilpena Pound in the Flinders Ranges. Isn't that great?"

Claire and Henry were met with blank stares. Rather than be over the moon, for the second time in as many weeks the kids surprised with their underwhelming reaction. Quizzically, Harriet looked at Lucy, who in turn looked at John, who in turn kept patting Freddy in between sneaking him bits of pancake.

Believing her parents had lost the plot, Harriet could not comprehend the news. According to them, one minute she wasn't studying hard enough and next they were taking her out of school for a holiday. Talk about hypocrisy. What sort of shitshow was this? "How can we? It's not school holidays," said Harriet.

"All taken care of, Harrie," said Henry smugly. "I phoned the principal and explained the situation. She's onboard."

Claire added, "With all that's gone on we think a short break is what we all need. It's only for five days but it'll be fun. Go and pack a few things and be ready in an hour if you can. I'll help John pack, but you girls can look after yourselves."

Harriet was about to make another mocking remark but swallowed her words as a thought bubble germinated in her brain. Five days off school could be cool, especially after the embarrassing one-goal loss in the netball final and her bungled effort to stop the opposing player who was instrumental in Glenelg winning. Fronting her school mates again had been preying on her mind. She'd gotten through the first week at school since the game okay, but she wasn't convinced everyone had excused her for her lapse in concentration. Some of the girls had stared at her strangely, but no one had given her lip. Harriet, however, didn't believe she was out of the woods just yet. She could still cop it!

It wasn't every day her parents pulled her out of school and took her on vacation. While Harriet slowly warmed to the proposition, there'd be no acknowledgement of appreciation. Not yet. It was just another one of mum and dad's crazy ideas that could work in her favour. At least on this occasion.

Lucy was also rather conflicted at the thought of missing school. The long Christmas break wasn't far away but getting in early with a bonus five days was cool. Not sure about camping in the Flinders Rangers but a holiday was a holiday. Still, she'd miss her friends.

Mulling things over in his head, John suddenly said, "Rangers! Are we seeing the Power Ranges?"

"No silly," said Harriet, derisively.

"You're silly." John fired back.

"Stop it you two," said Claire, intervening. "John, we're camping in the Flinders Ranges. You like camping. We build a bonfire, sing songs, play games and look at the stars in the night sky. All those fun things."

Grasping all those activities at once was a challenge for the six-year-old, John adding, "Yeah! I like camping!"

"You don't even know where we are going." Harriet's nose was out of joint and bickering with her younger brother was the remedy for her irritability. She could count on him to retaliate. Like clockwork.

"I do so," said John.

Claire had had enough of the fighting. "Harriet, no more! We leave in an hour. Hop to it, everyone."

Claire and Henry had the same thought. At least one of their three children was thrilled to be getting away. They also agreed that with hindsight they should not have sprung the holiday on the children at the last minute but given them more time to take it in. It was a lesson learnt. They were ready to leave in two hours. The car was packed, and they had enough food for five days. While most of the family were happy to go camping, Harriet was still frowning. Noticeably. The children were in the back seat and Freddy was on Lucy's lap.

The lengthy road trip was fairly humdrum. After leaving the city limits and the nearby hills, the landscape flattened, the highway north of Adelaide passing through brown, desolate terrain. To relieve the boredom, Claire provided a history lesson for the children about the Flinders Ranges. Predictably, the level of interest varied. From some to none. Wilpena Pound, Claire the geosciences' lecturer explained, was shaped like a bowl and the highest elevated peak was over eleven hundred metres. With its salt bush shrubs and wildflowers, the surrounding topography was generally flat. Flat as one of her pancakes, Claire joked, trying to prompt a laugh from the children, especially Harriet whose sour face had not changed since the trip was announced.

There were no takers, Claire failing to even get a smile.

Interrupting, John wanted to know what 'too-pog' meant. The girls laughed while Claire simplified its meaning. "It's a difficult word to say and spell, John. It means countryside, scenery, bushes and trees."

Nodding furiously that he understood, John was less than pleased with his sisters laughing. Harriet and Lucy could be meanies. They were always picking on him.

Wilpena Pound was around seventeen kilometres long and eight kilometres wide, Claire said, and near-by mountain areas contained fossils dating back more than 550 million years. Some of the planet's oldest fossils. The Flinders Ranges, for palaeontologists, was the ultimate fun park. "Jurassic Park's dinosaurs have nothing on this part of the world," Claire chortled. "Scientists believe it is the earth's oldest animal ecosystem. The marine life have been fossilised in the sandstone for a long, long time."

John's attentiveness spiked when Jurassic Park was mentioned. He loved the movie but was scared when the big dinosaur was chasing the people and they were trapped in the upside-down car. His eyes were hidden for that part. Every time.

Moving on from extinct creatures, present-day fauna like kangaroos and emus were also in abundance. While talk of fossils, marine life and shrubs didn't excite, the mere mention of kangaroos and emus had Lucy and John grinning. John was wildly excited and threw his arms in the air. Harriet was still the odd one out, retaining a dead-pan face.

Henry, focusing on the road, was impressed with Claire's knowledge of the composition of rocks. Mind you, it was Claire's bread and butter. As a lecturer in the geosciences, she knew much about the earth's history, the origins of the continents, oceans, atmosphere, sky, stars and life ... you name it. Often trying to engage him in talk about minerals and how the continents formed, Henry did his best not to look bored. It was Claire's passion. Not his. Like his children, his interest in the planet and fossils was at the lower end of the scale.

Concentrating on the road and the other traffic also took his mind off recent events. He had been badly shaken by the dreams, especially the one where he stabbed Lucy. Accidentally. Henry kept looking in the rear-view mirror to make sure Lucy was in the car and breathing. She was. The dream was horrid. Seeing Claire shaking like a leaf was also disturbing. The thought was hard to block.

It had taken a series of terrible dreams to rouse him from his inertia and to admit he had a problem. How big a problem was uncertain. Now questioning his recent theory that he was Jack the Ripper incarnated, why was he reliving the Ripper murders? A mystery for which he had no answers. The five days away was what Doctor Henry Evans had ordered. What Claire, his Florence Nightingale, had ordered. Much to Henry and Claire's delight, the drive was bereft of any arguments. Not uncommon even with a short car trip for the kids in the back seat to quarrel.

The fact the journey was much longer than usual, and no major fights had erupted was a minor miracle.

By five o'clock the family had reached their destination after a five-hour drive. A camping ground near

Wilpena Pound would be home for the next five days. They selected a clearing a reasonable distance from the next group of holidaymakers and set up camp. The girls had a tent to themselves while John would be with his parents in the second tent. Simple to erect, the canvas tents were for people with a love for the outdoors and little flair for understanding instructions. Harriet and Lucy, having pitched their tent before their parents, set about looking for firewood for the bonfire following a request from their father.

Freddy, who was on a leash, accompanied the girls. The last thing they wanted was for Freddy to become lost in the bush chasing a kangaroo, so Harriet had a firm grip on the lead, aware of his predilection for running off. Not that the family had any idea of what Freddy would make of the hopping marsupials if he came across one. Henry and Claire were initially unsure whether to bring Freddy along for the holiday, but decided it wasn't worth a fight with the children who would insist. As dogs could not be brought into national parks, they found a camping ground outside the park's perimeter.

The family had only been camping once before. Two years earlier they'd camped down the south coast and spent a week near Goolwa at the mouth of the Murray River where it connects with the Southern Ocean. Being summer and hot, they were repeatedly pestered by flies and mosquitoes. Days swimming at the beach were fun; the nights under constant attack were less so.

As summer was still some weeks away, the days were forecast to be warm but not outrageously hot. Just perfect! Repellent had been packed so Claire was confident there'd be no repeat of the disastrous Goolwa holiday. While not always easy to predict how the children would react, Claire was pleasantly surprised and thankful that Henry had agreed to take the week off as he was resistant to slowing down. Always too many patients and too many sick people to see. Her holiday suggestion was accepted. Straightaway. It brought an instant smile to her face and a spontaneous hug for Henry who seemed as astonished as Claire when he answered in the affirmative.

They had arrived at their campsite and everyone, outwardly, was in a good mood, even Harriet flashing the odd smile. The week, hopefully, would provide the rest and reprieve they all needed, for the older members of the family at least. There would be plenty of sightseeing, bushwalking and chatting around the campfire.

Two hours after arriving, the fire was roaring thanks to the plentiful wood collected by Lucy and Harriet. Only walking a short distance, their arms were aching with the number of big sticks they'd collected. Harriet's arms were particularly sore, as hers was a juggling act, holding the wood and restraining Freddy.

The first meal was a speciality. Claire had pre-prepared a pasta that required warming up, and not much else. Heaps of foil-wrapped garlic bread had been placed under the hot embers. The pasta was slowly reheating in a large pot at the edge of the fire. No one realised how hungry they were until the first whiffs of the Penne with a cheese sauce wafted around the campsite.

Henry and Claire were enjoying a pinot and it was lemonade for the children. Freddy wasn't forgotten. He was gnawing on a large, fleshy lamb bone that was a recent roast dinner left over. If there were a few kangaroos nearby, Freddy showed no interest. And he wouldn't for hours! The bone had his undivided attention.

Not much was said after the hungry campers had finished their meals. Tiredness was setting in after the long drive and tasty dinner and by nine o'clock everyone was ready to hit the hay. There was a conversation about what to do the following day with mutual agreement that a bush walk was the go. It was also agreed that Freddy would be tethered to a pole in the tent with the girls. They'd brought his wicker basket so he wouldn't feel out of place. There were no lights close by, so they relied on their torches to get around. The well-lit shower block was more than two hundred metres away.

Within minutes of slipping inside their sleeping bags, Lucy and Harriet were asleep while John, lying between his parents was also out for the count. Also surprising was John's acceptance that he would sleep in the same tent as his parents. Unlike Goolwa where his tantrum was one for the ages when he was told he'd have to sleep in his parent's tent, this time John did not put up a fight. Still cross with his unkind sisters for laughing at his 'too-pog' question, a night with his parents did not seem so bad. With John sleeping soundly, Henry leant over and kissed Claire goodnight before switching off the torch.

The start of the family holiday had begun well. Bushwalking was planned for the next day, and Henry and Claire were glad there'd been consensus.

The road was unfamiliar, but the girl kept walking. None of the houses in this part of town were recognisable. Soon, turning into a narrow alleyway, the number thirteen was signposted on the building. There was a tapping sound coming from inside. The girl was lured through a doorway. An irresistible force was dragging her in. Perhaps mummy and daddy were inside? The room was small and grubby. The wooden floorboards were dirty; the ceiling plaster was peeling, and a large crack snaked down one of the walls. A single bed was next to another wall, and tables and a chair were nearby. Over the fireplace hung a painting.

Where was she? Why was she here? Standing uncomfortably in this little room the girl wanted to leave, but the force held her. Intense. Overpowering. Her legs couldn't move. She was alone in the room. It was scary.

Slowly, the contours of a body began to appear. On the bed, a shadow. The girl was impelled to go closer to the bed. The figure started to fill out. The energy drew her closer until she was near the head on the bed. But there was no face. Just bloodied gashes. The girl stepped back in fright as the walls and the wooden floorboards turned red.

As the girl tried to flee, a lacerated hand from the bed grasped her arm, the person begging for help ... mercy. Though the grip was feeble, the hand would not let go. No matter how much she tried, the girl could not leave.

"Go away!" Lucy screamed. "Mummy, help!"

Struggling to free himself from his sleeping bag, Henry believed the torch was near the front of the tent but in the dark, he couldn't find it. "Fuck. Where's the bloody torch?" He unzipped his sleeping bag and lurched to the front of the tent. After pushing his backpack aside and more rummaging around the floor of the tent, the torch was soon in his hand.

The tent was illuminated.

Claire, halfway out of her sleeping bag, said, "Was that Lucy?"

"I think so." Henry unzipped the flap of the tent and made his way to where Lucy and Harriet were sleeping, with Claire tagging behind.

When they reached the children's tent, Lucy was out of her sleeping bag and crying.

"It's okay, darling. You had a bad dream?" Claire cuddled her daughter, while Harriet was murmuring in her sleep, Lucy's yell failing to fully wake her.

Sobbing between words, Lucy said, "Terrible mummy. The woman in the bed had no face."

"Mummy and daddy are here. Go back to sleep." Claire stroked Lucy's hair gently.

Henry wanted to know more about the dream. His daughter had been scared out of her wits but now was not the time to dig deeper. Henry wondered, however, what Lucy would remember in the morning. Did she have the same dream as him? The woman with no face. Probably just a coincidence.

With a reassuring cuddle from Claire, Lucy soon dropped off.

Chapter 8

The family had gathered around the campfire in readiness for the morning bush walk. Everyone but Harriet. Last out of bed, Harriet was still at the shower block brushing her teeth. While they waited for their eldest daughter, Henry and Claire decided they would ask Lucy about her nightmare. Lucy and John were bored and playing a game where they tried to push each other over. A game most likely to end in a fight so a distraction would be welcome.

"Do you remember me being in your tent last night? said Claire.

A big shake of the head from Lucy as she gave John another small shove in the side. "No. Were you in my tent?"

"You had a bad dream."

"Did I?"

"That's good," said Henry, who was quietly disappointed Lucy couldn't remember but happy she seemed in good spirits. The mere mention of a woman with no face had sparked his curiosity. And his concern.

Harriet soon arrived back at camp and further talk of bad dreams was put on hold. Lucy's nightmare wasn't raised again that day. Harriet's presence also ended the pushing and shoving by her siblings. A scornful glare from Harriet and Lucy and John backed off. With packs on their backs and Lucy holding Freddy by his leash, the family set off for their morning hike. Henry and Claire were hopeful they'd get two or three hours out of their children before boredom and the arguments set in.

They chose a fairly flat trail to minimise fatigue. Emus, kangaroos, echidnas and a variety of native birds were seen on the trek. While the number of animals didn't surprise, the absence of other hikers did. It was as though they had the whole park to themselves, making the experience even more spectacular. Five hours later the family returned to the campsite. Slightly exhausted, they all agreed the bushwalk had been fun. The next few days would include more walks on different trails.

The rest of the week in the Flinders Ranges went without a hitch. No more bad dreams and no more yelling in the middle of the night. The holiday was all about daily walks through the bush and fun nights around the campfire under the stars, John especially taken with the night sky. Occasionally, Claire would stop and examine some unusual rock formations. As she began to explain what they were the kids would either keep walking or talk amongst themselves. Henry would do his best to nod in all the right places, but Claire understood she was on a hiding to nothing as her work was of no interest to the family. But persist in educating her family about minerals she would.

As the week progressed, Harriet became a little more verbal and almost delightful to be around, but netball remained a taboo topic. The one-goal loss that caused a massive meltdown was a no-go area. Arguments between the children and the adults were at an all-time low, Henry and Claire reasoning more short getaways, much like the day outing to the beach, might be the way in the future.

Returning home late on Friday night they all agreed, while it was a fun holiday, their own beds were most inviting after five nights living in sleeping bags and tents. A hot shower before bed was also on the cards as the showers at the camping site trickled water which was lukewarm at best, so it wasn't quite the same.

They didn't feel that clean, their bodies speckled with red outback dust and dirt.

Once the children were in bed, Henry and Claire also retired but sleep was difficult to come by. Both read for a while, then put their respective books down. Disturbed by Lucy's dream on the first night of the holiday, neither could switch their brains off.

"Lucy said the woman in her dream had no face," said Claire.

"Her description has also been playing on my mind. I had a similar dream as you know."

"It has to be a coincidence, Henry. There can't be anything to it, surely!"

"I'd like to think you're right, Claire but ..."

"But what?"

"How many people have the same dream about a woman with no face. None of it makes sense." Henry rolled over; after struggling to relax, sleep was now beckoning. "I'm bushed."

"Sleep well if you can, darling."

Henry's belief he was Jack the Ripper was one thing, but Claire was now worried about Lucy. What if there was something more to these dreams? What if? What if? Claire laughed. What a load of bollocks! That a well-educated woman in her thirties was contemplating such nonsense. Really! They'd had a great holiday up north and Christmas wasn't far away. Anyway, Lucy had forgotten about her nightmare the following morning and couldn't even remember being comforted after she screamed.

It was now time for the family to reset and prepare for the year ahead!

Aldgate
Saturday 10 November 1888

Bertha Eckersley waited until her husband had left for work. It was seven in the morning. As it was a Saturday, she could expect him home in the afternoon but there was still time to do the required housework and, more importantly, write her journal. The record of her life that gave her the most joy. One of the few joys!

She was now more certain than ever that Aldrich was leaving the house in the early hours. It had been happening for weeks, often in the middle of the night, but for what reason she did not know. She was awake the previous night when she heard the front door close, and someone descend the stairs. It was not her imagination. Bertha was of sound mind; her sanity was not in question. Aldrich was deceiving her.

With dip pen in hand, Bertha opened to the first blank page after her last journal entry. She hesitated briefly, then began writing: Saturday 10 November 1888.

'It was frightful to think I was going insane. I now know that is not the case. For a time, I believed Aldrich when he said he never left the house after dark because of the undesirable people who frequent this area, but I now know that to be an untruth. Sadly so! Last night I most definitely heard the front door close. I lifted my head from the pillow and could hear the sound of footsteps on the stairs. I quietly made my way to Aldrich's bedroom and found his bed had not been slept in. I can't tell you the distress this has caused. My trust in my husband has been most gravely harmed. But what to do next is the question I find the most difficult to answer. While he has not been himself, if I try to raise the issue with him, he either ignores me or changes the topic. It is most disconcerting. I am at a loss as what next to do. In whom can I confide? I have no one. I seldom despair but I feel such loneliness. What is worse is that I can't see an improvement in Aldrich. He may be incapable of bettering himself. In my soul I know I am wedded to Aldrich for all time. I can only pray that the Lord hears my prayers and can deliver peace to my broken heart.'

As Bertha closed her journal and placed it in the top drawer of her desk, she began to cry. Not for the first time had one of her journal entries made her weep.

Henry and Claire were grateful that Michael Jenkins had agreed to see them that Monday afternoon. Unofficially. Old friends they may have been, but his time was precious as he was booked solid months in advance as many in his profession were in the lead up to Christmas. His deed was appreciated. They'd arranged to meet in a coffee shop two doors down from his North Terrace rooms.

"Hi Claire, Henry."

They'd been so preoccupied staring onto North Terrace from the large Bay window, they had missed their friend stepping into the coffee shop. The lunchtime rush had ended and only two other tables were occupied. A mother and her young daughter were seated closest to them, while two men in suits were quietly conversing at the back of the café.

"Hi Michael." Henry stood and shook his friend's hand. A case of déjà vu for Henry following their recent catch up. The pit of his stomach was churning.

Said Claire, "It's been a while, Michael."

"It certainly has but you're looking well, Claire." Michael gave her a brief hug.

"Coffee, Michael?" Henry asked.

"I'm fine, thanks. As I explained to Henry this is an informal chat. You understand, Claire. If a formal appointment is required, there is someone I can recommend."

"Totally get it, Michael."

"So, I gathered from Henry's call this morning that Lucy had a similar experience?"

"In the Flinders Ranges last week. I umm ..." Claire hesitated. "Lucy said she had a dream about a woman with no face." Claire shuddered.

"I see."

Henry added, "The dead woman in my dream was Mary-Jane Kelly, one of Jack the Ripper's victims. Perhaps his last victim. Her face had been shredded."

Michael Jenkins, the professional he was, did not disclose that Henry's statement had floored him. He continued to take in the details as if nothing out of the ordinary had been said. But it was unusual.

"I googled the Ripper victims after a couple of my nightmares and the last one was the Kelly girl. Poor lass was only twenty-five. She was the only known victim who died inside a house. The rest were murdered on the street," Henry said.

"This is all rather crazy. Forgive the word crazy because I don't believe you are crazy, Henry. After our brief catch up, I put your condition down to working too hard, but as for Lucy's dream. A coincidence! No one to my knowledge shares the same dream."

Visibly relaxing in their chairs, a burden had been lifted. Henry and Claire sought affirmation they were not mad, and Michael Jenkins had provided that reassurance with his heartening words. Telling him their little secret had also been liberating.

"And how have you been sleeping, Claire?"

"Well ... in between Henry's nightmares." Claire flashed a rueful smile in Henry's direction.

"The dreams may just go away which is what I said to Henry last time. Bad dreams aside, how was the holiday?"

"Great. We all had fun. I think the break came at the right time," said Claire.

"We needed a holiday." Henry concurred. "We wouldn't normally take the kids out of school with the main holidays so close, but this was a necessity."

They left the café ten minutes later. Henry had been reluctant to divulge his belief that in a former life he was the Ripper. How else could he know so much about the victims? Still, he was grateful to Claire for staying mum about his wild Ripper assertion. His belief that he was Jack the Ripper in a past life.

Before they left, hypnotherapy was mentioned in passing. Michael Jenkins threw it into the mix as a possible next step to recovery. Henry was horrified at the thought of being treated by someone swinging a watch in front of his eyes. Hypnotherapy had its place, but it wasn't a medical procedure that Henry would normally put his hand up for. Not that he expressed his misgivings to his friend. For now, Henry and Claire were earnestly hoping there'd be no more nightmares. Ideally, Harriet could let go of her netball loss and Henry and Lucy wouldn't suffer from any more bad dreams.

For all their sakes everyone had to move on.

Chapter 9
Aldgate
Monday 9 November 1868

Aldrich had spent the day walking around the local borough. Sometimes aimlessly; other times with clear intent. Hungry, he tried several times to steal a piece of fruit or bread but each time the local trader had been awake to his plan, eyeing him suspiciously. He wasn't naturally gifted when it came to thieving and the repercussions if caught could be drastic. A crime that once resulted in a one-way trip to the penal colonies.

Detained at least twice and not yet into his first year as a teenager, the stern lectures he received from the bobbies about the wrongs of stealing rang in his ears for days. Following the scolding there was a smack across the ear, sometimes two, and he was sent on his way and told to stay out of trouble. Or else.

It was a lesson Aldrich refused to learn.

His mother wasn't due home for hours, and even when she was home, there'd be little food on the table. Occasionally, a loaf of bread and a handful of meat slivers would appear, depending on her level of drunkenness and if he was lucky.

Often, Aldrich had to fend for himself because much of his mother's paltry earnings went on alcohol. It was her staple diet. Never fully understanding what his mother did for work, there was a naïve understanding that it involved being naked with another person. With strangers. Several times he'd walked in on his mother, bare-breasted, and with a man.

She yelled, and Aldrich left. Hurriedly.

His mother tried to expand his unworldly knowledge of sex when he was ten. A rudimentary lesson during one of her more temperate moments. A rarity. Aldrich had shown little interest but rather than offend his mother, pretended to take it all in. As he grew older, he understood his mother's talk about sex was more about humiliating him. Making him feel small. He'd come to realise that she hated men but needed them to survive.

So, when she was with a man, he had to be invisible. Not a sound could he make for fear of retribution.

Aldrich prepared himself for another night without food. Many times he had gone to bed starving, his belly aching. Was there a time his belly had been full? Not that he could remember. Tomorrow he'd be up early to see what he could scrounge. He would have to be smarter. As he lay in bed, he thought of the route he'd take in the morning. A long day on the streets it would be, but he was determined to satisfy his empty stomach.

Aldrich understood he would need to be cannier around the trader's stalls if he was going to eat. There were ways to distract the merchants. He had watched the street kids go about their mischief, so it was possible. But he'd need to learn fast. Street kids were shrewd, and they had to be to survive. Born on the streets, they toiled and played the grimy alleyways and backstreets to their advantage.

Considerations about his plans for the following day finally gave way to sleep. But his slumber didn't last long. Soon he woke. Recognisable. Disgusting. Chilling. The foul-mouthed breath was overpowering.

One hand was on his genitals. The stroking was gentle, but firm and he soon stiffened. He had no control. His body was not his own. The woman said nothing, but she was groaning, the bed squeaking in harmony with the gyrating hand on her pelvis. Her legs were pulsating. One of her knees dug into his back. Scared, Aldrich kept his eyes shut. Partly through fear, he was determined not to give the woman a face or an identity. Her body continued to quiver. The sound lingered. Deep and guttural.

After several minutes there was a high-pitch squeal and then quiet. She was motionless.

Just when he decided he could take no more, his body was his again. Despite the throbbing the spasm below his tummy also felt strangely nice, Aldrich wondering what next to do. Finally, the woman rolled off the mattress and landed on all fours. She used the bed to drag herself from the floor, staggered to her feet, grunted satisfactorily, and left his room.

Confused, Aldrich was sore from the constant rubbing. There was something else. His stomach was wet. He touched the skin below his belly button. Had the woman cut him? Was he bleeding? The sticky substance was new. Frightening.

Aldrich began to cry, softly. What had the woman done to him?

John always looked forward to Santa visiting on Christmas Eve. He was a passionate fan of the jolly fat man from the North Pole. John's annual wish list often spilled onto a second page, though mum and dad were at pains to tell him Santa couldn't possibly deliver on every request. Santa was a busy man and had many countries to visit and many needy children to satisfy. Top of John's Christmas wish list was a dinosaur called Rex which could roar like no dinosaur John had heard before. Rex could battle his other dinosaurs. The fights would be so much fun!

Harriet and Lucy were of the age they were aware who filled their stockings on Christmas morning but the delight on their faces, nonetheless, was unmistakable. Lucy requested a Barbie doll and a beach setting while Harriet was more interested in a face makeup set. She also threw in a beauty salon kit so she could play around with her hair colour. Her proclivity was for a lighter colouring.

The Evans's house was decorated at the start of December. While Henry was an apathetic contributor, Claire and the children doing the bulk of the work, he would do his bit. Sort of. The blow-up Santa on the front lawn and the reign deer antlers to hang over Freddy's wicker basket were tasked to him. There was also the wreath to attach to the front door. Hardly taxing, so no surprises that Henry never complained. Claire and the kids were happy to carry out the lion's share because they loved Christmas. The fact the family was jovial pleased Henry, who did not consider himself a Scrooge. That he took more of a ho-hum approach to the festive season; well, that was Henry!

Unlike decorating his own house, Henry enjoyed taking the family on a night-time drive around the neighbourhood to see how other people decked out their homes. An assortment of reindeer, rooftop Santas and gardens littered with life-sized snowmen dazzled the senses. In Australia, Christmas fell during summer, so the snow-themed decorations put up by some people was bemusing. Luminous snowmen with scarves, gloves and woollen caps were out of place. And the effort some people put into their Christmas lights was over the top. The homeowners' electricity bills would have been astronomical.

The annual Christmas lunch that included a smattering of cousins, aunts and uncles was always a grand affair, usually held at their home near the beach. Such was the size of their backyard it could host the entire neighbourhood. The weather was often warm so there was ample room for outdoor dining. However, if the mercury climbed too high, Claire would set up inside the house in air-conditioned comfort. One Christmas she attempted an outdoor lunch when it was too hot. Many of the foods melted in the heat, including the desserts which resembled a lava flow.

Claire vowed, "Never again!"

And because of the location near the beach, guests could drive the short ten-minutes for a swim if they wanted to cool off and if they hadn't overindulged in turkey, ham and pudding. Not to mention the champagne, beer and wine.

Claire tried to limit the number of guests to under twenty-five for Christmas lunch when she was hosting. A larger group and mild panic would set in. As organised as Claire was, smaller gatherings were more to her taste.

They were less hassle.

As Christmas came and went there'd been no nightmares. Claire and Henry were beginning to think the situation was an aberration, of what they did not know, but an aberration all the same. Jack the Ripper had taken a holiday along with most Australians. Which meant no need for a hypnotherapist. That was their current thinking. Henry and Claire, mystified as to the cause, were keen to consign that part of their lives to history. They were young and their children were young, so there was much to look forward to.

The year was ending on a grand note. The year ahead held promise of even greater things. That is, except for the children's arguments.

Like most holiday breaks, the longer they went the rattier the children became. They'd get bored and start picking on one another. Henry and Claire believed the Christmas holidays were too long. School break up was early December and the children would not go back until late January. By early in the new year the house resembled a warzone. Lucy and Harriet would argue, only to be surpassed by Harriet and John's quarrels. There'd be days all three would be at one another's throats. Henry and Claire juggled their holidays and minding duties so at least one parent was home with the kids.

Claire poured the hot water into the cup. She found her second cup of tea for the day was just as enjoyable as the first. As she sat in the kitchen sipping her tea, she wondered how long the house would remain quiet. There had been few issues and a rare tranquillity had descended on the home. Harriet, Lucy and John had been playing in their own rooms and Freddy was asleep in the hallway.

Claire had three more days alone with the kids. She was due back at work on the Monday so soon it would be Henry's turn. She placed her dirty cup in the dishwasher when there was a loud bang upstairs followed by a scream. It was John. The peaceful morning had ended. At least she'd been able to finish her tea.

"Okay, what happened?" Claire entered John's room to find him on the floor crying. "What's wrong, darling?"

"Mummy ... Harriet ... she ..." In between the sobs, John had trouble with his words. "She broke Rex."

It was then Claire saw the toy in bits on the carpet next to John. A Christmas present from Santa, the wailing, screeching T-rex was their son's pride and joy. There hadn't been a day since Christmas morning John had not had the dinosaur in his hands. It even joined him at the dinner table, much to Freddy's disapproval, believing the T-rex was scooping up food scraps meant for him. Rex had certainly seen better days. One arm was missing, and part of a leg was hanging by a thread. Despite his dismemberment, Rex could still roar and hiss loudly.

"Harriet, come here," yelled Claire. Not bothering to move from John's room, Harriet would have to explain herself at the scene of the alleged crime.

After hearing her mother call out, Harriet skulked into John's bedroom.

"You broke my dinosaur," said a tearful John, and pointing his finger menacingly at his sister.

"Well, Harriet. What happened?"

"It's so bloody noisy. I didn't mean to break it, but I could hear it all the way in my room. I can't hear myself think." Harriet knew she was skating on thin ice, but believed she had a case. Albeit a flimsy one. "I asked John if he could play with Rex downstairs, and he didn't."

"It's John's room. He can do what he likes," added Claire.

"I know but he makes so much noise."

"Your brother is six. What part of that age do you not understand?"

"I tried to grab the dinosaur off him, and it broke," said Harriet, determined to get a fair hearing. "It was an accident. Sorry John."

"You shouldn't have been in John's room grabbing his dinosaur in the first place."

"I know." Harriet turned from her mother and brother and rolled her eyes.

"You're not sorry," said John, still mad about his broken toy.

"We will fix your dinosaur, John. Harriet's apologised, as she should have." Claire explained how Rex would soon be brand new again, but it might take a couple of days.

Rex reappeared the next morning at the foot of John's bed with all limbs intact. Unbeknownst to John, the store replaced Rex at no extra cost. There had been numerous returns from customers after Christmas with the dinosaur's legs vulnerable to snapping off. John couldn't tell the difference and was just happy to have his dinosaur back.

In spite of his sister's nastiness or just to spite her, John played on the staircase with his prize toy all morning.

Rex's roar was louder than ever.

Chapter 10

The school year had begun positively for Harriet and the netball loss the previous year was now all but forgotten. Despite her fears, her teammates at the Henley Hawks had not given her a hard time. On the contrary, they had been very supportive. More than half the team were also her schoolmates. There'd been a couple of snide remarks about Harriet breaking under pressure, but the tactless comments had not come from her close friends. And they were not made to her directly but behind her back.

Harriet was her own worst enemy believing the world was against her and everyone was conspiring to make her life difficult. However, nothing could've been further from the truth. Her parents blamed her age. The problematic teenage years when any issue could seem like the end of the world. Puberty could result in youthful despair, dejection and hopelessness.

Harriet endured all those emotions, but rarely in silence. If she was miserable, she was sure to inflict her roller coaster emotions on her parents and siblings.

Now in her second year of high school, she'd been told by the teachers, as had the whole class in the first assembly of the year, that it was time to take their education seriously. Dedication and hard work would pay off in their final years at school with grades that could propel them into their career of choice. Doing the hard yards now would pay dividends later. A favourite refrain of the teachers. Harriet understood the reasoning, but the motivation just wasn't there. Besides, it was only the first week of the first term.

Sitting at her bedroom desk, she was more engaged with the games on her laptop. There were also stories to read about her favourite singers, the cute ones in particular. Learning about the Napoleonic wars or the dangers of inflation drew a monster yawn. History and economics could wait. She had all year to knuckle down.

By nine o'clock her day was done.

She brushed her teeth and went to bed. Having her own room was a blessing. Lucy could be so annoying, as little sisters could be, and as for John, he asked too many questions. Dumb questions. Conveniently forgetting her brother was only six, Harriet's intolerance for her siblings was legendary, her parents always harping about the age difference and asking her to be more patient. Harriet didn't care. They drove her mad. Harriet was the long-suffering family member. Not John or Lucy. She had to put up with so much. Her parents did not understand. They were too old and set in their ways.

No sooner had she dropped off than Harriet was in another world. No school. No pesky teachers. No homework. No annoying Lucy or John. No aggravating, stupid parents.

A place faraway where people dressed weirdly. Women in peculiar dresses that ballooned from their midriff down and men in top hats and long black coats. Many of the men had thick beards and moustaches that curled at the end. There were no cars, only carts pulled by horses. The streets were murky and grungy. The children were the same age as Lucy and John and had smudged faces and ragged clothes that emulated the grubby streets. Some were playing. Most were cheerless.

Harriet was walking along a road. Not a wide road like in Adelaide but bumpy and narrow. No one was around. She called out but no one answered. On she walked until she reached an alleyway. Stopping, she felt the need to go inside the building on the corner. A young child brushed past, almost knocking her to the ground. He giggled after the near collision but did not stop.

Harriet was now inside. The room was dark and mirrored the bleakness of the outside world. Slowly, the room became clearer. There was a fireplace, several small tables, a chair and a bed. A man dressed in a black coat and a hat was standing over the bed. He was pounding. Again and again. Wildly.

Harriet moved closer. She asked him, "What are you doing?"

The man struck the bed, his right arm hitting the mattress with brute force. Relentless. How weird, she thought. The man faced Harriet, but his face like that of the child was blurry. Without a word, he soon vanished.

From near the fireplace, the boy who almost knocked her over, was glaring at Harriet. Going by his size, she guessed he was no older than John.

"Go and play in a sandpit," she said, sternly.

The boy was annoying. He wouldn't say a thing. What was wrong with him? Harriet wanted to leave the room, but there were no windows or doors. Boxed in, the walls sloped at right angles and her feet slid closer to the bed. The bed where the stranger had been striking out. Ferociously.

The silhouette began to appear. There was someone lying on the bed. Harriet stepped back as the shape took a form. The room changed colour. Dazzling. Brilliant. A kaleidoscope of deep crimson. The room was splashed with a deep red. Harriet wanted to stay as she had never seen such beauty. So rich; so vibrant; so stunning.

The shape was no longer a shape, and the red began to fade, Harriet peering ever so nearer. It was a person, but it wasn't a person. There was no face. Just horribly grotesque cuts crisscrossing the head.

The walls and floor were soon covered in blood splatter.

Horrified, Harriet tried to get out, but her legs would not carry her. It was then she noticed part of a breast and an intestine on one of the tables. So much revulsion. Opening her mouth to scream, one of Harriet's arms fell from her body ... then a leg. She was trapped and bleeding profusely. How could she stop the haemorrhaging?

She yelled to the boy, but he faded into the fireplace. Like the stranger, he was gone. Harriet was alone. There would be no escape. The unfolding horror ....

Henry and Claire leapt from their bed, Harriet's blood curdling scream waking them in an instant. They raced down the hallway to her bedroom. The light went on. Harriet was standing on her mattress, her face ashen, her right arm slicing through the air.

Up and down. Up and down.

Believing their daughter was still dreaming, Henry and Claire each held a hand and coaxed Harriet under the covers. There was no struggle. She lay down and was tucked in by Claire, who then kissed her forehead and said, "It's okay sweetheart. You're in your own bed and mum and dad are here."

No more words were spoken, and Harriet's eyes soon shut, her face slowly returning to its normal hue. She hadn't been awake. Henry and Claire sat with her for another ten minutes before withdrawing to their bedroom, curious as to what had caused such an outburst.

This year was meant to be a new start for the family. The nightmares of the past year would be forgotten. Both dreaded that their daughter had also dreamt about the Whitechapel killer but for now their fears would be kept in check. They would prod Harriet for details later. Gently.

Hopefully more would be known in the morning.

Aldgate
Saturday 10 November 1871

Approaching his fourteenth birthday Aldrich was proud of himself. He had become more proficient at pinching food and other necessities. His life was fair, if not mundane, no thanks to his mother. He had managed to stay clear of the law in recent years and his deft handy work ensured what he wanted was what he got. His filching habits were too canny for the local traders. Even if he was seen in the act of thievery, Aldrich was too fleet of foot. Many of the traders were too old and too slow. Each day the routine was repeated. Attending a different part of the borough, Aldrich would assess several stalls for a possible weak spot. Lone traders were particularly vulnerable.

For one or two hours he would amble back and forward along the street, mingling with the crowds and trying to avoid suspicion. And detection. His preferred method of thieving as they passed a stall involved walking behind an elderly couple, casually, as if they were together. While the trader's eyes were elsewhere, serving a customer, he would snatch the produce and have it in his small carry bag in a flash. The trader was none-the-wiser.

His reflexes had become acute. Masterful.

While most street kids worked in pairs, Aldrich was a loner and preferred to work to his own schedule. That schedule did not involve other teenagers of his age. Aldrich had learnt to fend for himself since he was a little boy. His mother, a drinker who showed little interest in him, saw Aldrich as a millstone around her neck. That was made clear to him in her words and actions. They had forged separate lives for as long as he could recall.

At least her whorish behaviour, reckless as it was, had kept a roof over his head when he was young.

The weekly visits from her mother's friend had tailed off and were now more infrequent. Sometimes monthly. Sometimes every several months. Whether he was happy about the fewer visits or not, Aldrich could not determine. Perversely, he liked the thrill of the aftermath. Hearing his bedroom door open, he'd ready himself for what was to follow. Excitement. Anticipation. He would often stiffen before the woman got into his bed.

While her actions initially repulsed, the outcome was fulfilling. And while the bad breath was a battle, Aldrich took up breathing through his mouth, blocking the worst of her rotten breath. She'd moan and groan and do whatever while rubbing him, clearly relishing her handywork. He was eleven when he thought his life was about to end with the fluid on his stomach. That never happened and three years on he was still breathing.

Nowadays, the fluid would spurt. Effortlessly. Vigorously. Pleasurably.

While birthdays were never celebrated, Aldrich had a razor-sharp mind for dates, and could recount every mishap and bad deed that had befallen him. The year. The date. The time. At age eleven, when the woman had first touched him. The night his mother, naked, berated him for inadvertently walking in on her with a man. Evoking that early mistreatment caused the angst and hatred to build.

Once it had manifested with his treatment of a smaller child in the street. He had lashed out, hitting the youth with a solid punch to the ribs. For no other reason than the child had made a funny face at him.

Standing over the boy who was younger and watching him writhe in agony was pleasing. The domination gave Aldrich satisfaction. He much preferred being in control than being controlled. Too many times in the past he'd been bullied by his mother and people close to her. So, rather than contain his resentment, he encouraged it.

Emboldened by the rage, it was payback for those who'd wronged him or got in his way.

Almost dusk, it'd been a good day. He had pinched three pieces of fruit and a bread roll. After he'd had his fill, he wandered down to the corner of Dorset Road and Commercial Street and watched the women go about their business. All dolled up with red cheeks and lips to match, Aldrich viewed it as mildly amusing; the way they tried to outwit one another with their fancy words and swanky gestures.

They looked foolish. Fake. Like his mother.

Rivalry for the same clientele who were few in number some nights would result in the odd skirmish between the women. Those with a belly full of liquor were especially prone to fight. The conversation would start friendly enough. But a glare or wrong word and there'd be all out warfare. Punches, slaps and kicks. They'd roll on the ground providing spontaneous entertainment for startled onlookers who were forced to tip toe around the squealing combatants. A co-worker would sometimes intervene while on other occasions hostilities only stopped after one woman sauntered off into the night, nursing her hurt pride.

Listening to the women argue, Aldrich was mindful of the way the locals spoke. He had been aware growing up, but the older he got the inflections had become more obvious. He had heard the toffs from the other side of London speak after the occasional venture from the East End, but now as a teenager the distinction was stark. Aldrich felt shamed by his upbringing and how he spoke. No way would he end up like his bitch of a mother. He promised himself that one day he would be free of the East End ... free of the people, the grime and the way they talked.

In no hurry to get home where there'd be no warmth on this night like every other night, after an hour had passed Aldrich was bored. Retreating from the tiresome theatrics of the women, he set off along Dorset Road.

He soon turned off the main road and into an alley-way. A small tin rolled in front of him tapping his shoe, the likely culprit a cat resting on a carboard box ten feet away. Rather than flee, the cat stayed put, meowing. Aldrich stared at the cat, a tabby. Strange creatures. So many people kept them as pets. Why? He never under-stood.

He called to the cat, but it did not move. Shuffling slowly forward, the cat remained crouched on the box. Aldrich took several paces forward, but the cat stood its ground. Not a stray, Aldrich pondered, but some-one's pet as a stray would just take off. Now within arm's reach Aldrich bent down and picked the cat up. Tenderly. There was no effort to get away, the cat was seemingly happy to be in human hands.

Aldrich fondled the cat. Aroused by the long, deep strokes, his grip on the cat firmed. Aldrich applied more force. The cat struggled to get away and tried to scratch him.

Aldrich reached into his back pocket and pulled out a pocketknife. Flicking it open and without hesitating, his eyes glazing over, he hammered the knife into the cat's head. Once. Twice. Three times. The cat, with hardly a whimper, went limp. Aldrich hurled the cat onto the cardboard box. Wiping the small amount of blood from his hands onto his already dirty pants, he slipped the knife into his back pocket.

Aldrich licked his lips, reached into his side trouser pocket for the apple he'd pinched earlier in the day, and chomped. Hard.

Enjoying a coffee on the patio, Henry and Claire were up early. With good reason. There hadn't been any more blood-curdling screams from Harriet, thankfully, after the almighty scare she gave them during the early hours. Now that he had heard Lucy and Harriet shout in the dead of night, Henry better understood the terror such screams could exact on others. He had inflicted many a bad night on Claire with his nightmares about Jack the Ripper, a man detested for his heinous murders but for which he felt a strange connection. The gut-wrenching shrieks were enough to haunt even those with the hardest hearing.

Henry now had a clearer idea of what 'waking up the dead' meant.

"I hope Harriet is okay this morning," said Claire. "She was freaked out."

"We were all freaked out, Henry."

"She may not remember the nightmare. I think she was still asleep. I've read you shouldn't try and wake people if they're sleep walking. It's better to get them back to a natural state of sleep."

"That makes sense." Claire stopped midstream as Harriet strolled out the back door. "Morning Harrie."

"Hi." Pulling up a chair, Harriet sat. "What's up?"

"Not much. Mum and I are just having a coffee in the sunshine."

Harriet was not one for long conversations with her parents. First thing in the morning was always out of bounds. This would not be a long exchange, more of a 'How's your morning?' Then to her bedroom for a more fruitful talk on her phone with one of her close friends. She couldn't find much in common with her parents. They were all over the place with their whacky demands and how they ran the house. They always sided with Lucy and John. So unfair! They were to be left alone wherever possible. That was how she'd deal with her parents.

Before their daughter joined them, Claire and Henry had discussed how they'd broach the subject. Knowing their daughter's prickliness at times, they conferred over who would raise the nightmare with her. They wanted to know Harriet was okay. Nothing more.

There was a brief silence, then Henry began. "Harrie, did you sleep okay?"

"Yeah?"

"No bad dreams?" Claire asked.

"Nah."

"Nothing at all," said Henry, desperate for more than one-word answers.

"You two are so weird." Harriet got up. That was their good morning to her. Talking about her sleep and if she'd had a bad dream. Even when she tried to be pleasant, they would sabotage the chat with stupid questions. They had no fucking idea!

"This is serious, darling," said Claire. "You yelled out in your sleep, but you weren't awake. Dad and I found you standing on your bed. You looked ... well, you were terrified."

Harriet glared at her parents. Annoyed with the interrogation, she said, "I'll tell you what terrifies me. Your questions. I couldn't tell you what I dreamt or even if I did dream. I woke up fine. End of story."

"As long as you're fine," Claire said, diplomatically.

Harriet was back in the house before Claire and Henry could ask another question. "What is it with teenagers and not wanting to talk to their parents," said Henry, miffed at his daughter's uncooperative attitude. "Surely, she could sense our concern. We only want the best for her."

"At least she doesn't have any lingering issues from the dream," said Claire. "Or none that we know of."

"That's true enough."

"All three of us could see Michael." Claire was grasping at straws, but her desperation was building.

"No, Michael suggested a hypnotherapist, remember?" Henry was adamant.

"Then we take Harriet to a hypnotherapist. It might unlock something."

"I can't see Harriet agreeing to that. Our obliging, agreeable, responsive daughter," said Henry, tongue-in-cheek. "She'd never talk to us again."

"So many things we can't explain, Henry. Maybe a hypnotherapist would do you the world of good."

"Nah, not keen."

The idea of persuading Harriet to see a hypnotherapist didn't excite Henry. There had to be another way of dealing with the issue. Besides, neither he nor Lucy had had a nightmare for ages. Not one bad dream. Best to leave it alone. And after having a break over Christmas, he felt more refreshed. Laughing at his own silliness, how he ever thought he was the Ripper? Pure humbug. While he had poured cold water on that theory, concerns about Harriet remained.

"If I'm being honest, I'm a little worried about Harriet."

"How so?" said Claire.

"She's disagreeable about so many things."

"Henry, she's a teenager."

"I guess so. But I don't recall being so argumentative at her age."

"Perhaps you've forgotten, dear."

"My memory's not that bad."

Claire laughed. While clearly good at diagnosing health issues, her doctor husband could be unenlightened about his own daughter's mood swings. "Harriet will be fine. She's at an impressionable age. Just give her time."

Henry's mind soon switched back to the more pressing problem of the nightmares. There was a simple reason for them. Claire and Michael were on the money. He was overworked and needed rest. There was a logical explanation for everything. Henry was, after all, a doctor. There must've been a time, long past, when he read about the Ripper killings and retained the details. That could explain his fearful dreams.

But the question remained why Lucy and Harriet had had similar experiences. On that question Henry had no answer.

Aldgate
Saturday 18 November 1888

Bertha Eckersley's life had spiralled into a deep pit of unhappiness. Winter had arrived with a vengeance and recent Sunday outings with Aldrich had been cancelled because of the inclement weather. This day was no different. The weather was abysmal. A bitterly cold Artic wind was blowing strongly. Another Sunday inside the home with Aldrich, her husband who all but disregarded her. There'd be housework to do and preparations for the evening meal while Aldrich read. Little to look forward to. It was work during the week and then there were the weekends.

Such tedium.

Nothing could fill the void in her heart, a hollowness created by an uncaring husband who lied to her. It wasn't as if Bertha was afraid of Aldrich, but his temperament dictated the mood of the household. He never yelled but Bertha well understood if he was displeased. It was the scowl and his blackening eyes. Her heart was punctured by a profound sorrow. The journal entries of the past few months had the same underlying themes. Unloved. Joyless. Loneliness.

Bertha entered the loungeroom with feather duster in hand.

Aldrich was reading in his favourite chair. When Bertha appeared, he folded the newspaper on his lap and addressed his wife, "I have something important to tell you."

Aldrich's pronouncement surprised Bertha. He had been reading most of the afternoon without uttering a word and paying no heed to her comings and goings. And she had walked in and out of the room on many occasions. "Yes, dear." Bertha, as always, responded courteously.

"I've quit my job."

Bertha wasn't sure she'd heard her husband correctly and was about to ask him to repeat his comment, but Aldrich got in first.

"I've quit Bertha. Enough is enough. The work is uninteresting, and the weather is getting to me. I need a change."

Shocked by her husband's disclosure, Bertha said calmly, "How will we survive. We can't possibly live on my earnings, Aldrich."

"I understand Bertha. I'm not a complete fool. There's something else. I've lived in Aldgate all my life and it's a rat-infested hell hole. I was born here and lived under the same roof as my useless mother until I was fifteen ... and I'm still here."

Bertha was taken aback by Aldrich's eruption. Knowing that his upbringing had been tough and that he had no time for his mother, the gravity of what he had said still shocked. She'd long known that his mother had died in her forties and that Aldrich had raised himself, but as to all the specifics! One could only say they were a mystery as Aldrich was a man of few words.

"And another thing. I've booked two tickets on a sailing ship to the colonies. We're leaving England at the end of the month, so I would be well pleased if you could make the necessary arrangements and start packing for the voyage."

Startled that the initial surprise took an even more unexpected turn, Bertha was hushed in the middle of the room. She looked from Aldrich to the clock on the mantelpiece and back to Aldrich. Never in her life had she been so flabbergasted, and she wasn't sure whether it was the news of the impending voyage or Aldrich's directive to start packing that caused the most exasperation. But exasperated and lost for words she surely was.

Bertha began dusting the clock on the mantelpiece, the same clock she had dusted minutes earlier. The feather duster kept missing the clock, Bertha not concentrating on the task at hand. "May I enquire as to what I can take on this voyage?" she asked, with seething indignation.

"Whatever you like, Bertha. I don't believe there's a limit on personal luggage. Unfortunately, the furniture will have to stay. I'll see what I can sell before we go."

"Not even my desk. That has to stay?"

"Yes, even your desk."

Bertha was spinning. She would seek her journal as a matter of priority. An urgent entry had to be made. Writing her thoughts down would assist in comprehending what had transpired. Aldrich quitting his job? Moving to the colonies? What madness was this? "Well, there's much to do. I better write a list."

Reeling from the announcement, Bertha left Aldrich to his newspaper. As she sat, journal open on the desk in her bedroom, Bertha had two main thoughts. First, why her indifferent husband wanted her to travel with him abroad and second, amongst the confusion, she'd forgotten to ask where in God's name they were going. What colony? The Americas? And for how long?

On the upside it was charming that Aldrich still fancied her company. The man who hardly ever acknowledged her. But what had possessed him to make such an arrangement without consulting her? Beyond reasonable. Surely, she should be allowed a say in her future and where she lived. Not an unfair expectation by any means. While Aldrich could display unusual characteristics, injudicious and impulsive he was not.

Bertha sat longer than usual before penning the first words as her thoughts were scrambled. Nothing was clear to her. There was no flow. The words would not come; no matter how long she sat; no matter how much she toyed with the pen in her fingers. Something must have happened at Aldrich's workplace. But why the sudden need to travel abroad and leave their home? Challenging him would not achieve anything. He would go anyway. What then would she do?

Bertha was beside herself. This journal entry would be more difficult than most.

Chapter 11

Harriet always shunned her family at netball matches. Her explanation was simple enough. Acknowledging her family and friends, even briefly, during match time was not cool. It was all about winning the game. Bad enough hearing her parents cheering from the sideline. A maddening distraction. While approving of their interest, the encouraging shouts were embarrassing. Other families were also excruciatingly bad, their daughters sharing Harriet's misgivings.

Strong at intercepting, Harriet's position was goal defence. She had played that position from the first time she took up the game. Above average in height for her age, she had a freakish ability to know where the ball was heading, so her intercept skills made her one of the team's most valued players.

The match had been played at lightning speed, spectators oohing, aahing and living every throw, catch, intercept, pass and goal. The odd spill and tumble were also greeted with howls. The first three quarters had been dynamic. A game worthy of a final. With a quarter left and huddled with the coach at one end of the court, the girls were urged to stay the course. While the Hawks were narrowly in front it was imperative not only to defend strongly but continue to play attacking netball. Now was not the time to retreat into their shells and be defensive. Teams that play defensive, the coach stressed, did not win finals.

Fifteen minutes remained. A place in the grand final and possible glory awaited the victors.

Interlocking arms, the battle cry to be heard one more time, the girls yelled, "Hawks Fly Forever!"

With raucous hoots and howls, they dispersed, a fierce resolve exuding from every muscle in their collective bodies. They joined the opposition on the court who were already in their positions for the final quarter. The bell sounded. Game on. For 10 minutes Harriet's team held a two-goal lead. Goal for goal. Little separated the teams. The ball zipped from one end of the court to the other. Harriet had spoilt her opponent several times, but despite her best efforts the opposition was gaining the upper hand. With two minutes to go, the Hawks faltered.

Both teams were now equal on forty-two goals.

Less than a minute left on the clock and the opposition had possession. The ball travelled quickly down the court towards Harriet and her adversary. Anticipating, Harriet jumped high to her left, the ball inches from her fingers, but she could only watch, helplessly, as her arch-rival in goal attack faked a move forward only to double back and grasp the ball. Her eyes darting around the court, the ball criss-crossed from goal attack to the goal shooter. Hushed. For the first time in the match the crowd was deathly quiet. One of the teams was positioned on the cliff top, perilously, and soon to topple over the edge.

Which team?

From a metre out the opposition goal shooter, who towered over the other girls, steadied and guided the ball high in the air. As soon as the ball left her hands it was never going to miss, and it dropped effortlessly into the net. The bell sounded. Half the crowd went berserk, the rest fell silent.

The Henley Hawks were out of the competition. Devastation.

Fatigued, numb and near tears, Harriet slumped. Her anguished teammates also dropped to their knees, despairingly. A one goal loss. To have the match in the palm of their hands, only to let it slip. Unbelievable. There were hugs and sobs amongst the girls as the coach sprinted onto the court to console the team.

Diverting her gaze from the Hawk's supporters, Harriet trudged over to where the triumphant opposition players were still jumping for joy, hugging and kissing. Scenes of pure bliss. Seeking out her rival, a girl she'd played on many times in the past, Harriet offered her hand, her parents drilling into her from a young age the importance of being a good sport.

The girl smiled, appreciative of the gesture. Stepping back, Harriet saw blood on the girl's cheek seeping from a wound above her ear. It was a large slit. Harriet saw mum and dad approach with Lucy and John in tow.

"The girl is bleeding. We need to help her."

"You bet we do," said Henry.

"Of course, honey," Claire added.

The girl did not speak. Soon, blood was gushing from a gaping wound to her head and her white netball dress turned the colour of a tropical sunset. Horrified, her teammates rallied around. The girl's face was raw, layers of skin shedding, bits of membrane falling onto the court.

"Mum, Dad, what are we going to do?" Harriet was hysterical, the girl who had won the netball match was dying in front of her. She was the hero and heroes don't die at the age of thirteen. It just doesn't happen.

"Where's her face? She has no face." Harriet wailed, before collapsing with her family around her.

Michael Jenkins reached for the sugar jar and added two teaspoons to his coffee. He stirred, slowly, and took a sip. "Too much sugar, I know. I need to cut back." For whatever reason, he decided his sugar consumption required an explanation.

"Thank you for coming, Michael," said Claire. She was not at all interested in the amount of sugar he had put in his coffee but was desperately appreciative that he'd made the effort to visit at short notice.

Waiting for an explanation as to why they needed to see him, Michael Jenkins perused the backyard. "The weather is starting to turn. I see the leaves are browning and falling to the ground."

"Not the leaves on the gum tree," said Claire, pointing to the branches of the large eucalyptus tree that was a dominant feature of the backyard. And as for the patio, it's wonderful for a drink and a meal as long as it's not raining or blowing a gale."

"So, I gather there was another incident last night," Michael Jenkins said, forsaking the small talk and cognisant his Saturday morning had to include the weekly grocery shopping.

Said Henry, "Harriet had a nightmare this morning. She's had two now and screamed the house down both times. When we went to her bedroom last night she was standing on her mattress, white as a ghost. Similar to an incident weeks ago."

"Tell me more."

"The dream caused such a commotion that not only did she wake us, but Lucy and John also flew out of their bedrooms. She was standing up on her mattress, trapped in a Twilight Zone of sorts," said Henry. "The dream was about a netball defeat, but it was the manner of her rival's death, the way Harriet explained it. Having no face and blood draining from her body had an all too familiar ring. The ring of a Ripper killing."

Interrupting, Claire said, "We've never discussed the Jack the Ripper murders in front of the children. None of them."

"Or who Mary-Jane Kelly was or Black Mary, Dark Mary, Fair Emma and Ginger." Henry rattled off the names in succession. Unheard of before the nightmares began, they were now well-known to him. Sadly so.

"Those names belong to?" said Michael Jenkins, unknowingly.

"Mary-Jane Kelly was the last known victim, but she also went by the other names I mentioned. She must have had an issue with alter egos," joked Henry.

"That's your diagnosis, Henry?" said Michael Jenkins.

All three laughed.

"I was revolted by her death in my own nightmares. Though differing in content, our dreams panned out the same," Henry said, reflectively, and quick to move on from his joke.

"Both times Harriet was standing on her bed and moving her arm up and down as if striking out at something. The first nightmare she couldn't remember a thing but last night she could," Claire said.

"She was almost comatose after the first dream but not this time. Thankfully, she calmed down quickly. All this on top of Lucy's nightmare in the Flinders Ranges," added Henry.

Michael Jenkins sipped his coffee. As he put the cup down Harriet came out the back door.

"And here is the girl of the moment," Henry declared.

"You remember Dr Jenkins, Harriet." Claire decided an introduction was necessary as they hadn't seen one another for several years.

"Hello," Harriet said, coyly, finding a chair next to her father.

"Call me Michael, please."

Harriet patted Freddy on the head. He was camped at her feet after following her outside. If Henry and Claire thought their daughter would clam up in front of their psychiatrist friend, they were wrong. Their usually stroppy, high-spirited teenage daughter was a willing participant. No defiant stares. No growly noises. They had pre-empted his visit that morning and Harriet agreed to speak to him. The latest incident was terrifying, so she was keen to talk about her experience.

Michael Jenkins began, "I don't want this to be traumatic for you, Harriet, but what can you tell me about your dream?"

"I remember the game we lost and the girl I was playing on. She stole the ball out of my hands and held onto it for too long. With seconds to go, she passed it up the court, and they goaled. We lost! I should have been given a free pass."

Harriet had a unique way of rewriting history. That wasn't how Henry and Claire recalled the last seconds of the game, believing Harriet was outplayed fair and square but they stayed mum. The conversation was not about the netball loss but the dream.

"I went over to congratulate Marcie, that's her name, but she had no face. Well, she did to begin with and then she didn't. It vanished. Bits of her face were coming off on the court and blood was everywhere. It was horrible." Harriet shuddered.

"And the first dream is a mystery. No memory?" asked Michael Jenkins.

"No," said Harriet. "I don't remember mum and dad coming to my room, but I remember them last night."

"And the poor girl's face just fell away?" said Michael Jenkins, seeing the distress in Harriet's eyes.

"Yeah. The whole thing was so revolting! Can I go now?" Harriet had no more to say. She'd already put her nightmare down to her inability to accept the preliminary final loss. It stung. It stung more than anything else.

"Yes, sweetheart, off you go," Claire said.

"Nice meeting you again, Doctor ... I mean, Michael." Harriet corrected herself, happy to use a first name and not a more formal title.

"You to, Harriet. Take care."

With the backdoor closing and Freddy following his daughter inside, Henry said, "One thing I didn't tell you when I last visited. And I didn't want to say this but with Harriet having these dreams it may be important."

"Go on, Henry."

"As I explained at my first appointment, ahh catch up, I researched all the Ripper killings and relived them in my dreams one-by-one. The last killing of Mary-Jane Kelly was particularly horrid. Mutilated. Terrible state of affairs. I told Claire and she thought that was a crazy thing to say but I honestly believe ... believed ... that I was Jack the Ripper in a past life. Stupid, I know. Don't judge me please, but that was what I thought."

There. Henry had unloaded with his Ripper theory. Probably embarrassed himself but a necessary disclosure considering the latest incident involving Harriet. Strangely, he felt happy with what he'd said. He had finally got it off his chest.

Michael Jenkins sat impassively.

Finishing the last of his coffee, he said, "Henry, you are not Jack the Ripper, not even in a past life. Of that, I'm sure. What is disturbing is that you and your daughters have had similar dreams, witnessing or seeing a girl who has no face and has been butchered. Whether that girl is Mary-Jane Kelly, Black Mary, or Little Red Riding Hood, I don't know but that I also doubt. Even families that are close, and I know you guys are, don't have the same dream. Our minds process things differently and it's next to impossible to have the same dream ... I've never heard of it anyway."

"So, it's official. We're all going mad?" Claire said, lamentably and hoping her family wasn't disintegrating.

"No, Claire, not for a minute are you going mad. I can recommend a friend of mine who is a hypnotherapist. She might be better placed to unlock these dreams. I'm not an expert in this area and while mental health issues, stress and spicy food can lead to bad dreams, there could be more to this. That's my unofficial judgement."

"Hypnotherapist, eh?" said Henry, quizzically. "We'll try anything."

"Okay, I'll pass on her details."

"Fantastic. It's worth a try," said Claire, convinced her family had unresolved issues but perking up after hearing of the fresh strategy.

Henry and Claire believed they had no choice but to seek further help. Their daughters, particularly their thirteen-year-old, needed protecting. Harriet was entering her formative years so safeguard her they would. Whatever it took.

Three months earlier

Harriet had never taken an interest in her family garage. What was stored there was of little relevance.

Junk. Dust. Bugs. Which is why she surprised herself one afternoon when her parents were shopping, and she was charged with babysitting John and Lucy. John had requested Harriet watch a Disney movie with him. An emphatic no from Harriet. Lucy had asked Harriet to play a board game. An equally emphatic no. Harriet was cross because her friend, Milly, had asked her to see a movie. She had to decline. Her bloody parents had stifled her independence ... again.

Quietly fuming about her ruined Saturday, Harriet wasn't about to sulk in her bedroom.

Fed up with everyone and everything, she would sift through dad's stuff in the garage. If she was bored stiff after ten minutes, she'd move onto another project. It wasn't the type of building depicted in old horror movies with cobwebs hanging from the ceiling. Thankfully, the small number of cobwebs weren't visible as the garage was in relatively immaculate condition. Her father was a neat freak. Boxes were tidily stacked on top of one another in one corner of the garage while tools on hooks hung in the opposite corner.

Heading straight for the boxes, several were moved out of the way. Impatiently. Eyeing a container wedged between two boxes at the back and partly covered by a white sheet, Harriet pulled the sheet back revealing an old brown trunk. The leather casing was in good condition, but the nails, screws and hinges were rusting. Badly.

The discovery intrigued Harriet.

No padlock. Great. Easy entry. Hoping to find valuables like jewellery or money, Harriet tugged the top of the trunk. Stubbornly stiff. After two hefty jerks the trunk opened with a loud screech. But early excitement gave way to disappointment, the trunk all but empty except for an old hat, a scarf and a book. How annoying! What a shit!

About to move to another box, Harriet paused. Something fascinated her about the book. She flicked through the pages. It was in remarkably good condition. Old writing. One date read: 19 January 1890. She flipped back to the front. The name 'Bertha Eckersley' was inscribed on the inside front page.

Harriet considered the name. Harriet couldn't recall any previous mentions of this person by any family member. Then again, she may not have been listening. As a rule, old people and old places had no appeal. They were long gone and didn't impact her life. Nothing to see here.

Hesitating, she was about to place the old book back in the trunk when the thought crossed her mind that the document might be handy if her class had a show and tell down the track. You never know! First, she would ask her parents who Bertha was. Someone famous! A distant cousin or an old aunt that nobody liked! More likely.

The afternoon hadn't been a complete waste after all. As she left the garage, book in hand, she heard John calling from inside the house. Damn the babysitting role. Because she was the eldest child. Parents could be such a pain. They were no fun! She wasn't even being paid to babysit. Outrageous! This would be the last time she'd agree to mind her brother and sister. In future they could look after themselves. Entering her bedroom and still irritated about missing the movie with Milly, she was gobsmacked to find Lucy cross-legged on her bed.

"What are you doing, Lucy?"

"Nothing."

"Who said you could come into my room?" Harriet was incensed.

"I was looking for you."

"You can't come into my room unless you're invited. Got it!"

"I'm bored," said Lucy, hoping to extract sympathy from her older sister. "I want to play with you."

"Well, I don't want to play with you. Go and play with John."

"He's too much of a baby."

"Just leave, Lucy." Harriet was in no mood to argue. "I've got things to do." Harriet approached her bed with increased frustration as Lucy showed no signs of shifting. Younger sisters could be such a pest, especially hers. "I won't tell you again. Leave. Now!" Harriet was getting angrier.

"Don't want to." Lucy began playing with her hair, all but ignoring her sister. Without warning, Harriet lunged at Lucy shoving her sideways off the bed. Unprepared, Lucy hit the floor hard, bottom first. She howled. More from fright than pain.

"I told you to get out. It's your fault," said Harriet, whose guilty conscience at losing her cool was not about to be shared with her sister.

"It's not my fault." Sobbing, Lucy picked herself up off the floor and made for the door. "You're so mean, Harriet. I hate you."

"The feeling is mutual. And close the door on the way out!"

Harriet sat on her bed as Lucy limped from the bedroom. Harriet's Saturday had gone from bad to worse. One thing she knew for certain. Lucy would be ready and waiting to spill the beans as soon as her parents walked in the front door. There'd be another almighty shitshow, so Harriet had to think of a good excuse.

Plymouth
Friday 30 November 1888

The date for Aldrich and Bertha's departure from London had arrived. The month had quickly passed. Aldrich had taken care of most of the arrangements, including selling the furniture, while Bertha was left to pack the trunks. Saying goodbye to London's East End was not a cause of heartache for Bertha or Aldrich. Especially Aldrich who let it be known of his displeasure for the area where he had spent his entire life. He had instigated the move; Bertha was invited to follow.

And follow she did.

After her initial disapproval at Aldrich for not consulting her, she had become increasingly attached to the idea of a change. Penning the words in her journal on the day he declared his intentions helped, as she tried to work out Aldrich's motives for wanting the move. Her husband's edict was acceptable to Bertha.

Neither expressed regret nor sorrow, though it was still unclear to Bertha whether she'd ever return to England.

Leaving from London's Paddington station, the train trip to Plymouth, a distance of 190 miles, took about five hours. Plymouth, the seaside port, where they would bid farewell to England. Neither Aldrich nor Bertha had ever seen the sea so the sound of the waves, splashing on the nearby beach had them spellbound. On the sandy foreshore, their faces dampening from the drifting sea spray, there was time enough to be hypnotised by the breaking waves as the ship was not setting sail for six hours. Bertha took off her boots and bathed her feet in the icy water, Aldrich doing no such thing; his boots were fastened to his feet.

While still flummoxed by the suddenness of their exit, Bertha's life had hardly been much to rave about, so any lifestyle change was welcome. An opportune time to reset her marriage with Aldrich. After minor contemplation the only thing she would miss was her large oak desk. The same desk she'd spent many hours sitting and writing her journal. A chronicle that had become her most intimate companion.

Aldrich sold the desk and the other furniture for a pretty penny helping to pay for the voyage. That, along with the money they had saved, ensured they could travel second class, Aldrich not settling for anything less. After a wretchedly poor upbringing, Aldrich was determined his adult life would be more comfortable, less miserable.

They were booked on the 222-foot clipper, Torrens, captained by Henry Robert Angel, who proudly claimed to anyone within earshot that the three-masted ship was the fastest clipper to travel the Plymouth to the Port of Adelaide route. A man in his sixtieth year, his weathered, ruddy face, long white beard and large stature were in keeping with the ruggedness and unpredictability of his profession. The high seas were not for the weak or faint-hearted. The ship sailed to Australia via the Cape of Good Hope several times a year, but the voyage would not be without its dangers as the seas could be treacherous, the southern tip of Africa, infamously so.

A notorious graveyard for ships.

A week out from Plymouth and Bertha could not recall ever feeling so ill. So sick she could barely leave her cabin. From day one after departing England, Bertha suffered from sea sickness. Dreadfully. There wasn't a day she could keep her food down and most of the voyage was spent prostrate in her cabin. Her stomach pitched in unison with every roll of the wave; her head so light there were moments she believed it would simply float away.

Taking only first and second-class passengers, Aldrich and Bertha were told the voyage on the Torrens, on average, took seventy-four days. With Bertha feeling the way she did that was seventy-four days too many! Aldrich, however, had no such qualms. He ate two hearty meals a day without any misgivings, Bertha deciding he had a cast iron stomach. Meals consisted of corned beef, mutton, salt pork, potatoes, rice, tinned carrots and soup. Bread and biscuits were also offered to the passengers.

While his wife had to confine herself to her cabin for much of the voyage, Aldrich spent many daylight hours topside, strolling back and forth along the deck, enthralled by what he saw. Aldrich watched the crew for hours: from the boatswain who shouted orders at everyone, to the seamen who handled the rigging and the ropes and the general maintenance. Duties were carried out with precision, Aldrich admiring their efficiency.

His powers of observation had always served him well.

In his fifteenth year, Aldrich had begun walking into the centre of London Town to study the people and watch how they acted, talked and interacted with others. He had long had a dislike for the way East Enders spoke. It grated. The dialect gave a person's place of birth away in an instant. One day a week Aldrich made the foot journey to Leicester Square, Drury Lane or Piccadilly and waited. He would stand and watch.

As a well-to-do couple passed, he would follow at a safe distance so as not to arouse suspicion. But not so far away that he couldn't hear the couple chat. Pronunciation of certain words and how they expressed themselves with their hands were important. After many months, Aldrich believed he had all but mastered the fundamentals, and could pass himself off as a middle-class Londoner. The only give-away were his tatty clothes. That was something he would need to work on.

Later, when he found work as a stonemason's apprentice, his appearance was instrumental in him being offered the job. That, combined with a fresh look, courtesy of a new shirt and a decent pair of pants that he'd nicked from a clothes shop. There were skills he was destined never to lose. But while his talents to observe and imitate were not in question, embarrassingly, he still could not read and write.

Self-conscious of this weakness, he soon landed on his feet again.

Several weeks into his apprenticeship, one of the more experienced stonemasons realised that Aldrich's literacy skills were non-existent. Charlie, who'd been in the trade for thirty years, took him under his wing. He took a liking to Aldrich. Having had a tough childhood himself, Charlie saw some of himself in the sullen, guarded teenager who was slow to trust. With many of his teeth missing but with a smile as wide as the Thames, Charlie had been charged with guiding Aldrich in the finer points of stonemasonry, so tutoring him in reading and writing was not an issue.

After a little cajoling from Charlie, Aldrich began daily reading and writing lessons. Much to Charlie's surprise, there wasn't a day Aldrich was late. He would arrive at six in the morning. On the dot. With no formal education, Aldrich didn't want to be held back. Like the middle and upper classes and speaking well, reading and writing were critical if one was to advance in life.

A fast learner, within a year Aldrich had progressed sufficiently to read newspaper articles. Writing took longer but Charlie was nonetheless impressed by Aldrich's aptitude for learning. He knew from the outset he was a bright kid but like many of the children in the area, he had been neglected, and the opportunities had not been there.

Even though they were second class travellers, Bertha and Aldrich were asked during the second week at sea if they'd like to dine with Captain Angel, but his hospitality was gratefully declined due to Bertha's feeble condition. Only one invitation was forthcoming during the voyage. A shame. Because Captain Angel, according to the cabin crew was due to retire in a year or so and his tales of past voyages were legendary. A man who regaled his guests for hours on end with yarns of heroic survival against cyclonic winds, 100-foot waves and giant sea creatures.

Captain Angel's stories could've come from the annals of Moby Dick. But unlike Ahab's misfortune, Captain Angel's long legs were intact. There had been no wayward encounter with a large, white whale and no limbs were missing. While his maritime skills were exemplary, embellishing the truth was a small blemish on his otherwise commendable and genial personality.

His dinner guests never complained; his every word was gold. Captain Angel was a splendid raconteur.

For several days the Torrens sailed within sight of the southern continent, the passengers' early glimpse of this alien land. On the seventy-eighth day, the Torrens sailed via the Backstairs Passage around Kangaroo Island before making its way to the Port River. For the past week the wind had been light, the waves calm. Though regularly bragging that the Torrens was the fastest clipper of its generation, Captain Angel conceded it was not the swiftest trip and was thirteen days shy of its fastest recorded time.

Nonetheless, Captain Angel was well pleased with himself and his crew. In the fifteen years he'd captained the Torrens there had been no major incidents. Not one. When the clipper finally berthed, there were roars of approval and three spontaneous cheers for the captain. A narrow tidal estuary winding between mangrove swamps and marshland, at low tide in the colony's early days there was a risk of becoming stranded in the shallow waters of the Port River.

But after sections of the river were dredged, ships running aground were a rarity.

To set foot on dry land again was to Bertha's immense relief. What she didn't care much for was the heat and the flies. Having next to no knowledge of this new colony and its climate, after disembarking she was attacked by flies, the likes of which she had never encountered. It felt like hundreds had stuck to her face and clothes or flew around her like bees around a beehive and no amount of swatting or swiping made an iota of difference.

Inscrutably frustrating. The flies were desperate to socialise with humans.

And to make matters worse and as she was outfitted for an English winter, the perspiration droplets appearing on her forehead soon became a steady stream down her face. The moisture on her face was a magnet for even more flies. Bertha had never identified with such discomfort; the thick corset, long dress and woollen shawl incompatible with local conditions. One bonus. Her favourite straw hat festooned with artificial flowers kept the searing sun off her pale English face.

A small mercy!

After so many sick days at sea and despite the heat and the flies, Bertha was grateful they had arrived.

Safely. Horse-drawn coaches were queued in line ready to take the Torrens' passengers to their respective destinations. After retrieving their four large trunks, the coachman with a thick Irish brogue told Bertha and Aldrich the City of Adelaide was a journey of almost eight miles.

A ride on a dirt track taking no more than an hour.

Once the coachman had secured their luggage on top of the coach they settled into their closed carriage. Just to be out of the sun was a blessing. An air of nervous excitement swept over Bertha. Would she be safe in this new land? Could they make a living here? Would the new start be good for her husband? So many unknowns. Daunting. Discarding her shawl, Bertha instinctively reached for Aldrich's hand.

To her utter amazement and her delight, he accepted.

The first month in the new colony was eventful for Aldrich and Bertha, if not demanding, as the search began for accommodation and work. Bertha's forebodings about their future security were compounded by a collapse in property prices and growing public distrust in the banking system in Australia. After a period of untold prosperity, including property booms and gold rushes over the past thirty years, a severe recession was on the horizon. The signs were worrying.

Their landing in South Australia had come at the worst possible time.

After arriving in the city from the Port of Adelaide they booked into a hotel in Grote street in the centre of the city where they spent their first month. The one-bedroom lodging was at the cheaper end of the market, but the downside was the shared bed, and for a couple used to separate bedrooms there were instants of awkwardness. While Bertha still had warmth for her husband, her sexual yearnings for Aldrich had diminished somewhat.

Bertha usually retired before her husband each night. A deep sleeper, she barely knew he was in the bed and was oblivious to his tossing and turning. Also, blissfully unaware of any wayward arms or legs in the middle of the night, Bertha's sleeps continued to be peaceful. Serene.

Their time at the hotel and sleeping arrangements proved to be acceptable. Bertha believed the conjugal rights of her husband had to be considered, but thankfully Aldrich did not make any distasteful or iniquitous demands. Moody and disagreeable he could be, but demanding when it came to the bedroom he was not. Bertha, not for the first time in the life of her marriage, was appreciative.

Reprieve from the hotel accommodation arrived with the purchase of a small cottage in East Terrace on the city's fringe. With the money left over after paying for the voyage, they put down a deposit on the recently built cottage. With two-bedrooms, a kitchen and a dining area it was adequate as their everyday wants were nominal. The cottage was complete with an outhouse in the backyard, their sanitation needs also covered. Bertha was jubilant with their new home. Aldrich, though not as effusive, expressed a similar sentiment.

While unemployment was rising, Aldrich found work as a stonemason. Sandstone was the brickwork of choice because of its unlimited supply in the nearby hills. Adelaide's population of around 150,000 was projected to grow in the decade ahead, despite the depression gripping the country. New homes had to be built. Many. Aldrich's proficiencies as a stonemason were much sought after and would be for years to come.

Bertha soon followed her husband into the local workforce finding a position as a seamstress in a backyard garment factory not five minutes' walk from their home. It was ideal. With the current work situation dubious, Bertha was delighted to find work. As was the case in London, her part-time earnings supplemented her husband's wage. Just as importantly, it got her out of the house several days a week.

Though times were tough, food was cheaper than London, so money spent on market day went a long way, with staples such as tomatoes, spinach, potatoes, beans and onions plentiful. The stalls were always full of local produce, the colony having long been self-sufficient.

Three months after arriving, Bertha and Aldrich had set themselves up. Nicely. The decision to leave London, while taken in haste, was now paying dividends. The weather was also more hospitable. Contrasting to the day of their arrival and the heat and the flies, the cool wintry temperatures were far more tolerable. Even the cloudier days, unlike London, did not seem as dull.

The light in this sun-drenched continent was somehow brighter.

As the weeks in their new home passed by, Bertha noticed an improvement in Aldrich's temperament. A small improvement but improvement there was. A dark veil had lifted. Aldrich was not as surly, and he began to smile more. The Sunday strolls also extended to Saturdays. Still, chitter-chatter between the pair was mixed, Bertha almost always initiating talk and with varying success. Dinner could be especially testing with Aldrich content to eat in relative silence before retiring to his bedroom to read the newspaper.

A convention that began long before Adelaide.

It wasn't the only practice from England to be continued, with Bertha reviving her journal writings that regrettably had been on hold during the long sea voyage. Her chronic sea sickness and proximity to her husband prevented any worthwhile writing. The daily inscriptions had been missed. Soon after moving into their East Terrace cottage her journal took precedence.

Once again.

Aldrich didn't start work as early in Australia. The previous job necessitated a seven o'clock start but with his new role his day began at half-seven or eight.

Bertha began her seamstress duties an hour later so her mornings routinely involved thirty minutes of jotting down her feelings from the preceding day. Once Aldrich had one foot out the door, Bertha swooped on her journal and had pen in hand.

While not romantically or sexually coupled in the traditional sense, thoughts of babies were never far from her mind. Conflicted, her biological clock was ticking and if they were going to start a family, it had to be soon.

New country. New home. New job. A family. That was her thinking.

Emboldened by her husband's improved manner, Bertha felt the conversation about having a baby could happen soon, her pluck increasing by the day. Raising the topic with her husband. Um. A delicate conversation it certainly would be, Bertha knowing she'd need to show sensitivity and diplomacy. Resolving to make her wishes known to Aldrich during one of their upcoming daily walks, it was a case of now or never. As the thought of never did not sit comfortably with Bertha, her mind was made up.

She wanted a baby.

Chapter 12

Harriet had many friends. Through her school and the local netball club, the Henley Hawks, she could not call herself a loner. Not by any stretch of the imagination. Most weekends her friends were texting, messaging or calling her; a small detail she tended to overlook. Despite this reality, Harriet complained that she was Miss Unpopular and maybe it was time to look for another school. Dismissing Harriet's assertions, her parents wouldn't have a bar of that argument.

The fault, according to her parents, lay with adolescent assertiveness and the onset of puberty. Never to be swayed or convinced that she wasn't being over-the-top, Harriet had an opposite view. Just mum and dad being boorish again. They were kill-joy parents. Pure and simple.

As it was too early in the year for netball, the season opener still a month away, Harriet woke in a horrible mood. Saturdays should've been fun. Every teenager basking in the knowledge that it wasn't a school day. No teachers. No classes. But not Harriet. She'd had a dreadful week at school with modest exam results in economics and biology, so Harriet wanted to stay in bed and scream into her pillow. Seeing or talking to anyone was out of the question. Her laptop and smart phone would occupy her day.

Throw in pop music and a movie or two and her Saturday was taken care of.

The altercation with Lucy had played out its final scene with Harriet apologising. The severe reprimand from her parents included home detention. Harriet would not be able to leave the house the following Saturday. Harriet had the right to ask Lucy to leave her room, her parents said, but pushing her off the bed was not okay. Lucy was only ten and Harriet being the older sibling by three years should have known better.

Harriet grimaced.

The 'older child should have known better' conversation. Knowing it was coming, Harriet did her darndest not to roll her eyes and answer back. She was itching to argue the point but knew from past experience that it would only make matters worse. Lucy was asking for it as she refused to leave her bedroom. What else could Harriet do? Reason with a sister that wasn't open to reasoning. How can you be rational with a ten-year-old? Initially ropeable with the penalty, Harriet knew she'd gone too far. So, the idea of spending a Saturday in her room took hold after the ten-minute chastisement from her parents.

There was also the journal she'd found in the garage. She could spend hours reading the various entries. What she'd skimmed, initially, was curious, the language in parts stupid. She gathered the woman didn't get on too well with her husband. In one entry, she said, 'I do worry so about Aldrich. I can only assume he's having difficulties at work, but he refuses to say. A stubborn man if ever there was one. On occasions he makes me feel wretched, so miserable.'

What sort of name was Aldrich? She had never heard of anyone called Aldrich. Harriet laughed. The old days made her laugh. Then again it was 19th century England. One thing that did not make her laugh, however, was the journal. Fascinating. But not funny.

The writings of Bertha Eckersley, to Harriet, read like a sad tale of loneliness and despair. Must have been depressing for people in bad marriages back in the day. No television, radio or iPads to stave off the boredom. The poor woman! Strangely, reading about Bertha's life made Harriet feel better about herself. A kinship had developed between generations. There was loneliness and then there was real loneliness. Bertha did not have a happy life. All considered, Harriet now believed her life wasn't so bad, after all.

Harriet decided to read the notes in chronological order. Concealed under her pillow for several weeks, she had been slow to start reading the journal. Now only up to July 1888. Harriet hoped beyond hope that Bertha's life would turn around. She'd planned to speak to her parents about Bertha and where she fitted into the family tree, if indeed she did, but was not on great speaking terms with either parent.

The rebuke after her fight with Lucy had only added kerosene to the fire. Her parents were being bloody nuisances. Again.

There was also their obvious disappointment in her exam results. Mum and dad had rubbed salt in the wound by claiming she could put more effort into her studies. Those comments were not helpful, though Harriet had to concede she could do better. Lately, her parents had been most annoying, and Harriet was content to keep communication with them to a minimum. The bare minimum.

No other conversation would Harriet entertain. She was in no mood for polite chitchat whether it be about her dreams or the weather.

Harriet had enjoyed a morning of relative peace. Lying on her bed, between reading diary excerpts, there had been a movie, YouTube music and a short nap. Text messages from girlfriends had gone unanswered. After another YouTube song, she opened Bertha's journal and despite an earlier undertaking to read the diary in chronological order, she moved forward several months in 1888.

Harriet's parents had individually knocked on her bedroom door during the morning to check that she was still in her room. Sighing deeply, her curt response on both occasions was, "Still here."

Aldgate
Saturday 10 November 1888

'It was frightful to think I was going insane. I now know that not to be the case. There was a time I believed Aldrich when he said he never left the house after dark because of the undesirable people who frequent this area, but I know that to be an untruth. Last night I most definitely heard the front door close. I lifted my head from the pillow and could hear the sound of footsteps on the stairs. I made my way to Aldrich's bedroom and found his bed had not been slept in. I can't tell you the distress this has caused. Trust in my husband has been most gravely harmed.'

Harriet was now captivated by this Bertha person, whoever she was. The relationship with her husband was going pear-shaped, heading south at the rate of knots. Harriet had to learn more.

'I am at a loss as what next to do. To whom can I confide? There is no one. I feel such loneliness. I seldom despair about my situation. What is worse is that I can't see an improvement in Aldrich. He may be incapable of improving. In my soul I know I am wedded to Aldrich for all time. I can only pray that the Lord hears my prayers and can deliver peace to my broken heart.'

Fully engaged with the read, but with her eyes drooping, Harriet was about to continue when there was a knock on her door. Early afternoon, Harriet was unmoved. Refusing to budge from her bed after the first knock, there was a second, more purposeful knock. Her bloody, disruptive parents were at her door again. How many times could they check on her in one day?

Harriet responded. Grouchily. "Who's there?"

The voice was soft. "Milly."

Harriett, still in her PJs, raced to the door. "Milly. So sorry. I thought it was mum or dad."

Milly hugged her friend. "All good, Harrie. I tried texting and calling you, but I guess you're not in the right mood today."

"I woke up feeling uugh! I thought I'd be a lousy friend so best to stay away from everyone." Harriet was now feeling guilty that she hadn't replied to the text messages. "Hope you understand. My family are being so unreasonable right now."

Milly sat on the bed. "Yeah. I know what that's like. All good. But I wasn't going to let you get away with doing nothing. Come on, get dressed. I have plans."

While Harriet was tall for her age, Milly was shorter with red hair and a slightly crooked nose. And despite Harriet complaining about friends, or lack thereof, Milly was attached to Harriet at the hip, as only a best friend could be.

Ignoring text messages just wouldn't do, Milly had to see for herself how her friend was travelling. They'd known each other since grade one. They bonded from the start. Their first shy encounter on the swings at a playground. Two squealing six-year-olds calling on their mothers to push them. Higher and higher. Their competitive natures were evident from an early age.

"So, what do you have planned?" Harriet had dressed in minutes, her mood improving after Milly's unexpected arrival.

"You wait and see Harriet Evans. All I'll say is that it involves the beach and ... boys!"

"Boys." Harriet's eyes bulged. Wildly. "Milly, you're a life saver. Love you so."

"Love you more."

"Give me a minute to change." Harriet, all but forgetting the parental ruling to stay indoors for the day, went to her wardrobe and skimmed the dresses on the clothes rack. One by one, she browsed each dress. The minute boys are mentioned and there's a strong desire to wear a pretty dress. Why? Milly had the right idea. She was wearing jeans and a floppy top. Harriet's eyes shifted to the chest of drawers and the pair of jeans tossed on top. She pulled on the jeans and brushed her hair, haphazardly. "Ready."

Looking her friend up and down, Milly stood. "You'll pass."

Both girls laughed.

"Thanks," said Harriet, grateful she had a bestie like Milly. "Oops. Need to loo. Hang on Milly!" Harriet made for the bathroom. While still early afternoon the day was overcast. The bathroom was dimly lit so Harriet flicked the light switch under the mirror, but the globe had blown. The ceiling light also didn't work. What the fuck! How could she check her face and hair in the mirror when she couldn't see.

This was a job for her parents. Surely, they could keep the lights on in the house. That's what parents were for. Not her job. Not John's. Not Lucy's. Bloody hell! Harriet unlocked the bathroom door and twisted the doorknob, but it wouldn't budge. She kept turning the handle but nothing. Now the crappy door wasn't working. First the lights and now the door.

The house was crap. Falling to pieces.

"Milly, can you open the door please?" Harriet hoped Milly would hear her pleas for help as her bedroom was closest to the bathroom. "Milly ... I can't get out. The door is stuck. Can you open the door for me." Harriet's tone was desperate. Why couldn't Milly hear her? She was in the next room. This was crazy. Harriet tried the door again. Still no luck. "Milly, for god's sake let me out of the fucking bathroom."

Just then the ceiling light began to flicker. Three times on and off. The bathroom dimmed further. Harriet became frantic. The bathroom had darkened to the point she could not see the hands in front of her face. Harriet thumped the door. Again. Again. Again. "Milly, please. Help me!"

Harriet slumped against the door and cried. Why was no one listening? Not her parents. Not Milly. Why was she being ignored? So unfair. Suddenly, the bathroom brightened. There was a sound from behind the shower curtain. Tap. Tap. Tap. The curtain was pulled across, and a man in a dark coat and clenching a long cane appeared. There was a black feather in his hat. Slightly taller than the stranger, Harriet was distracted for a fleeting moment, the feather proving an oddity.

"Who are you? Why are you in my house?" said Harriet, putting on a brave face.

The stranger approached. Intimidatingly. He said nothing. The tapping of the cane echoed on the tiled bathroom floor.

Tap. Tap. Tap.

"Mum, Dad .... help, there's someone in the bathroom," roared Harriet. "Come quickly."

From under the man's coat a knife appeared. The colour drained from her face. Harriet jumped up and twisted the door handle, but it was useless. She was trapped with nowhere to hide. The stranger touched her arm; his fingers were icy.

"Leave me alone!" Harriet screamed. Furiously turning the doorknob, the door flew open. Harriet took to her heels yelling for help as she hurtled down the staircase. Her friend Milly was all but forgotten. The house was empty. Harriet ran into the kitchen, her head swivelling from side to side like a clown's head at a carnival sideshow. What next? Escape to the patio? She heard the stranger coming down the staircase. From one of the drawers, she pulled out a serrated barbecue knife and pointed the blade at the kitchen door.

"Mum, Dad. Help!" Harriet was desperate. Still, no one was hearing her cries for help. She'd have to fend for herself. As the stranger entered and with the knife held shoulder high, Harriet lurched at the man. "Stay away," she shrieked. She swung the knife wildly through the air.

"Harriet, it's okay."

Her mother's welcoming words were heard through the fog of terror. "Mum." Harriet was being held, someone had hold of her arm.

"Sweetheart, put the knife down." Henry gripped his daughter's arm. He slowly prised the knife from her fingers, careful not to cut himself on the jagged edges.

"A man is after me. Why didn't you hear me?" Harriet had to protect herself. She was aware she was no longer in the kitchen but standing over Freddy's wicker basket in the hallway. Quivering, Freddy looked at her forlornly. "Why am I here? I was in the kitchen being chased."

"No darling, you were in the hallway screaming at Freddy. There is no man," said Claire, delicately. "You were standing over Freddy holding a knife."

"Freddy?" Harriet was confused. Bursting into tears, she bent down and cuddled Freddy. "Oh Freddy! Did I scare you?"

Henry and Claire first knew something was amiss when they heard John's cries. He had been down for an afternoon nap when he howled from the top of the staircase. Henry was in his office, and Claire was washing in the laundry. That's when they heard the screams. Harriet was screaming. They arrived at Freddy's wicker basket. Simultaneously. Harriet was standing, menacingly, over Freddy with the knife. Afraid she was about to strike their pet, Henry had managed to take the knife off his daughter who was in a somnambulistic state. She was asleep, but her eyes were open.

"Is Milly still here?" Harriet recalled her friend arriving and saying they'd meet some boys.

"Milly's not here," Henry said.

"She was here. Sitting on my bed. The man was in the bathroom. Then he chased me to the kitchen."

"Who darling?" said Claire.

"The man in the coat. I've seen him before. He scared me. Fuck, what's happening to me?" The tears rolled down Harriet's cheeks. Her life was a mess. Her mind was a mess. "... am I imagining all this shit?"

Such was their concern for Harriet's condition, the swear words were overlooked, neither parent batting an eyelid. Or caring. Almost inconsequential in light of current events. Henry would've believed his daughter was delusional except he had had similar, bizarre experiences.

Claire knelt and placed an arm around her daughter while Harriet sat in the wicker basket cuddling Freddy. Henry and Claire were heartbroken at seeing their daughter's predicament. Her cheeks were puffed-up from the tears. Michael Jenkins was going to put them in touch with a hypnotherapist, but they had yet to hear back from him. Or were they going to contact him for the details? Neither Henry nor Claire could remember. They were at a loss. Henry hadn't been keen on hypnotherapy, but he was quickly changing his mind. Something had to give. The torment had to stop. Henry and Claire had always known what to do where their children's health and wellbeing were concerned.

Not now. They were out of their depth. They needed professional help.

The incident in the hallway had rattled Harriet's cage. She was scared out of her wits. Her version of events didn't stack up. She now accepted there was no stranger in the house and no Milly. She wasn't being chased. Having dozed off on her bed, the next thing she remembered was threatening the family pet with a knife in the hallway. She could've seriously hurt Freddy. Everything was so fucked!

Petrified after another inexplicable episode, she realised that she needed mum and dad in her life. If anyone could help her it was her parents. They had spent two hours in her bedroom consoling her to a point where she felt protected. She felt loved. Isolating herself from her family was not the answer. While her relationship with her parents and her siblings had been rocky, at dinner that night Harriet decided to open up about the diary she'd found in the garage. She had been meaning to ask about it. Now was the time.

Harriet was the last family member to appear for dinner. She pulled up a chair between Lucy and John. Freddy was in his usual crouching position near John's legs and had his head pressed to the edge of the table. Knowing what Harriet had gone through that afternoon, her parents and siblings felt they needed to show their love and support.

Harriet had everyone's attention. Smiling broadly, she said, "Guess what?"

"What?" said Lucy, who was again on good terms with her sister after Harriet had apologised.

Touching Lucy's arm, Harriet said, "I found an old diary in a trunk in the garage."

"Wow," said Lucy, not understanding why the find was so important.

"Wow." John repeated, clueless as to what a diary was.

"Who wrote the diary?" Claire inquired.

"Someone called ... Bertha Eckersley," said Harriet, as if she were announcing the name of a competition winner on live television. The only thing missing was the drum roll.

Henry put down his fork and spoon. "Bertha Eckersley. Well, there's a blast from the past."

"Who is she, Henry?" Claire was now hooked.

Addressing Harriet specifically, Henry said, "Bertha Eckersley was your great-great-great-grandmother." He paused, then said, "I think I got that right. She and her husband, I believe, arrived from England sometime in the 19th century."

Henry had never been much interested in his family's history, but as a child he recalled his father talking about their great-grandparents. He knew of the trunk's existence because he accepted it from his father, reluctantly, shortly before he passed away, but to his knowledge it had only been opened the once. "What's the attraction of an old journal, Harrie?"

"I found it by accident. I've only read a few sentences here and there, but she sounds really sad. She didn't like her husband. Not much, anyway."

Claire hesitated, then said to Henry, "Did she have a hard life, dear?"

"I don't know much about their lives except they came from London. I remember dad saying their arrival coincided with a severe economic downturn. Things were tough but they both had jobs and survived the recession or depression, whatever it was. Thankfully, otherwise I might not be here."

Harriet set the journal down on the kitchen table next to her father. "I want to read more but it's boring in parts."

Laughing at Harriet's remark, Henry picked up the diary and went to the first page. "Bertha Eckersley. I think she outlived her husband by many years but as to her final resting place, of that I'm not sure. Somewhere in Adelaide, I guess."

"You should have paid more attention to your parents when you were younger, Henry."

While Claire shared Henry's apathy for family trees, she at least could trace her lineage, name many of her dead relatives and their place of birth. Henry, on the other hand, was ignorant of much of his family's ancestry, never showing an interest in anything that was older than him. And as for fossils and minerals, Claire rarely discussed the intricacies of her work in front of Henry knowing that cavernous yawns would follow.

And to be fair, she realised that early earth was not everyone's cup of tea.

"My father wasn't overly fascinated in our ancestry either," said Henry, looking to deflect the criticism. Why was it a crime to not have an interest in your relatives, especially those that had long passed? They'd had jobs, families, and in most cases, had done well in difficult circumstances. But it was all in the past. End of story. Pausing, Henry considered his next comment. "There was something unusual about Bertha's husband. Dad said he was odd, but I can't recall the exact circumstances. He'd been dead many years before grandpa was born. I don't even remember his name."

"Well, Bertha had trouble with him," said Harriet, taking pleasure in the fact she had begun the family discussion. "And I know his name. It was Aldrich. What a shocker of a name!"

Harriet howled while Claire and Henry chuckled. Lucy and John, their bowls almost empty, laughed loudest. Not knowing what the joke was, if their older sister found it funny, they also found it funny. They were in it together!

"Aldrich is an old, rather distinguished English name. It will probably make a big comeback one day. Most names do," said Henry, authoritatively. "You'll see."

"Not in my lifetime," said Harriet, sniggering.

Henry got out his smartphone. "Listen to this. Aldrich means old; wise; ruler. And the name has been around a long, long time. There you go."

Harriet wasn't moved. "I don't care. I still think it's an arse of a name."

"Harriet!" said Claire, challenging her daughter's poor choice of language.

"Oh mum! I only said arse. That's not a swear word. Chill."

The mention of arse and Lucy and John lost it. Completely. Arse was the naughtiest of words.

Seeing her younger sibling's faces redden the colour of a beetroot, Harriet could not help herself. In a slightly accented English voice, she repeated, "Arse. Arse. Arse."

Soon all five were in stitches, the raucous hoots and howls temporarily drowning out further conversation. Henry and Claire couldn't remember a time Harriet had laughed so long and so boisterously. An antidote for her recent stresses. It was so good to see. The family stayed around the dinner table for another hour, sharing jokes and more laughs.

Unbeknownst to John, during the hysterics Freddy had helped himself to a strand of spaghetti that had fallen onto his shorts and continued to lick John's pants long after the pasta had been devoured. Unbeknownst to the others, feeling guilty about her treatment of Freddy, Harriet had also fed him; three strands of her spaghetti somehow falling to the floor.

Adelaide
Saturday 21 September 1889

Finally, the day had arrived. While penning her deliberations a day later was her usual practice, Bertha was up an hour earlier to start writing, anticipating the possible outcome. Her hopes were rising. Aldrich was still in his bedroom. Weekend walks for Bertha and her husband, unlike their time back in London, were far more pleasurable. More than six months after arriving, Aldrich's mood had improved, markedly, and while many locals were struggling with the economic downturn, they were doing just fine. Aldrich's job as a stonemason was keeping him busy but the money was welcome. Enjoying her part-time job as a seamstress, life for Bertha was not as muddled as London.

Their new home was proving less complicated and more agreeable to the sort of lives they wanted for themselves.

Bertha was confident that her once unsociable, dour husband had made the right decision to leave England. This particular Saturday morning, early as it was, her mind was clear. Unambiguous. Taking up her dib pen she wrote:

'As is our normal Saturday practice, Aldrich and I will stroll to the East End Markets near North Terrace to replenish our fruit and vegetable supplies. It is a routine that even to my astonishment Aldrich has come to like. I find it charming that the markets are called East End, the same name as the area where Aldrich and I hail from in London. Not that Aldrich has fond memories of the area where he was raised. The names of many English towns and villages can also be found in Adelaide, Goodwood and Dulwich to name a few. These past months have been the most enjoyable of my married life. My prayers have been answered and I now have a husband who, though still likes to keep to himself much of the time, is now more inclined to consider my feelings. A minor miracle but a miracle it is! Today, I will pluck up the courage to talk about my needs as a wife and my desire to be a mother. I deserve to be heard and respected. I pray to God that Aldrich who has been more amenable to my longings will listen to my proposal with the good grace it warrants.'

Bertha left enough space at the bottom of the page for the outcome, whatever that outcome would be. That part of her entry would be added later. Bertha and Aldrich spent longer than usual at the markets. The morning sun had brought out large crowds and the fruit and vegetable stalls were bustling with activity. After buying the weekly essentials, they made their way back to their East Terrace cottage.

A short distance from home Bertha turned to her husband. "Aldrich, I need to talk to you. Something of great importance has been occupying my mind. For some time. I fear if I don't say it now, I never will. The moment will be lost." Bertha was confident in what she was about to say. She had to be.

Aldrich, resting against the wooden fruit cart, was quiet.

"You have a good job with the quarries and I'm earning as a seamstress. For months now I have considered our new life here and what it would mean to me, and you, if we had a ..."

Aldrich was silent. If he knew what his wife was about to say he didn't pre-empt her.

"What I'm trying to say is that I would love to have a baby. Our baby." Bertha hesitated, watching her husband with enormous intent. "The timing is right." Bertha calmed at once, unshackled from months of worry.

When his wife had finished Aldrich began to walk. After taking five short steps, he looked back at Bertha, his voice was gentle. "If that is your wish then it is my wish."

"It is my wish, Aldrich. It is very much my wish." Bertha was ecstatic. It was the response she had hoped for. Smiling broadly, she looped her arm in her husband's and together they strolled toward their home, Aldrich lugging the fruit cart.

After they'd reached the front gate, Aldrich addressed his wife. His tone was conciliatory. "One thing I must ask, Bertha."

"What's that dear?"

"When you give birth to a girl we will call her Mary-Jane."

Bertha considered her husband's request. She had thought of many boy's names, believing she'd have a boy. Girl's names had not been in the mix. "Mary-Jane. Is that a name close to your family?"

"No. But it's a name I would like for our daughter. I must insist on Mary-Jane."

Aldrich dragged the fruit cart into the house, Bertha left at the front gate to mull over Aldrich's demand. How extraordinary. Why on earth would Aldrich be so insistent on a name? And why was he so sure they'd have a girl? Bertha followed her husband into the cottage. She smiled. It did not matter. There was no point arguing over girl's names because Bertha believed she would have a boy.

Later that evening as Bertha was changing into her nightgown, Aldrich's request played over and over in her head. 'If that is your wish then it is my wish and when we have a girl, we will call her Mary-Jane.' Aldrich's dictate that they call their baby Mary-Jane was soon forgotten as Bertha was happy he had agreed to start a family.

Bertha had long accepted her husband's sullen deportment and his odd requests. As disconcerting as they were, she desperately tried to understand him. As she got into bed, her nightgown fitting loosely around her shoulders, another strange conversation was recalled. She didn't give it much credence at the time. On a recent weekend walk, Aldrich made a comment about the city's apparent lack of prostitutes.

The remark was made with an approving smile.

One of the things he liked about Adelaide was the sparseness and cleanliness. Not at all like London's smutty East End, he told Bertha. She had never given much thought about women who made money taking care of men's needs. How they conducted themselves was of no concern to her. Many were deprived and had no choice. That she understood, so she was not going to hold herself up as judge, jury and executioner. Aldrich, however, had a deleterious view about women who turned to prostitution.

Bertha believed Adelaide, like all cities, had underground brothels. She had been told Light Square, on the other side of the city to their residence, was patronised by those poor, unfortunate souls. The city, she'd been reliably told and despite her husband's belief, had more than its fair share of prostitutes. The younger women at her workplace would fill her in on the more sordid aspects of the city's night life. Bertha was all ears as she was open to broadening her education.

Aldrich and Bertha lived on East Terrace, a residential and quieter part of town. Did Aldrich perceive the city to be something that in reality it was not? Perhaps he had convinced himself that was the truth. Bertha let slide her husband's comment about the city's purity. If he was happy with that thought, then so be it. A less sombre husband was what Bertha had longed for. Indeed, what she had prayed for.

Bertha grinned. There was a noise outside her door. Further consideration of prostitutes was quickly forgotten. Two knocks. Unlike years past when the knocks were to satiate his needs, this time it was different. Aldrich was present for Bertha and to realise her wish for a baby. Suitably aroused thanks to her husband's positivity, Bertha believed it would be a most satisfying evening, her nightgown sinking below her shoulders as Aldrich entered.

Bertha's dream of starting a family, with God's blessing, would come to fruition.

Chapter 13
The Spitalfields
Friday 12 March 1880

The woman was terribly lost and running late for her appointment. This part of London, the East End, was formidable. The maze of narrow streets and laneways and the children with dirty faces, and the unemployed men on street corners stalking women with their lustful stares. Many of the people had foreign accents and understood little English. This was not an England she knew well. While unsure of the time, she believed it must've ticked past nine o'clock. Becoming frantic, she saw a well-attired man in a long black coat holding a cane on the other side of the street. He could be of assistance, so she made a beeline to him.

"Excuse me sir, I'm looking for the haberdashery on Commercial Street."

The man tapped his cane on the pavement and eyed the woman, dubiously.

"I'm most unfamiliar with this part of London, you see," added the woman, candidly. "I could use your help."

She did not look like the other women in the area. Appropriately dressed and not at all ornamental. And certainly not like the women who earnt their living by selling themselves; the ones with the caked-on lipstick and fluorescent cheeks. Concluding she was of good stock, he finally replied, "The haberdashery on Commercial Street. I believe I know the premises. Let me escort you."

The stranger's tone was formal but mannerly. The woman would not normally go off with any man, but her options were few and she was late. "Thank you but if you point me in the right direction, I'm sure I'll find the place."

"I insist," said the man, cordially. "Please, this way."

As he strode off, she felt obliged to follow. After recently being laid off at her previous job in Lewisham, she needed the work. She would travel to any part of London for ongoing employment. The haberdashery was less than a mile away and soon she was outside the three-storey factory with the stranger by her side.

There had been little communication between the two during the twenty-minute walk, the woman struggling to keep up with the man whose stride was as long as his cane. Courtesy of the stranger, she was also pleased to learn that she wasn't late at all. The man gave the time as two minutes to nine o'clock. Precisely. She was on time, after all.

"I can't thank you enough. It was very kind of you to show me the way." The woman did not want to seem rude, but she was eager to be punctual for the interview. "I must go, but again, thank you."

About to enter the haberdashery, the stranger called after her, "If you're free tomorrow night, I would be pleased if you would join me for dinner."

The invitation came as a surprise as the woman was halfway through the door. "Dinner." The man with the thin moustache was handsome enough, but the few words that had passed his lips gave very little away. She didn't know him. "Dinner," she repeated, as if the invitation was asked in a foreign language.

"There's an eating house not far from here, further along Commercial Street. It's called Abigail's. We could meet there at seven o'clock."

Coincidentally, the woman was staying with a friend not a mile away. Considering his dinner proposal for a third time, she said, "Yes. Seven o'clock would be suitable." About to disappear inside the haberdashery, she added, politely, "I don't even know your name, sir."

Allowing a thin smile, the man said, "Madam, my name is Aldrich Eckersley. Pleased to make your acquaintance ... and you are."

"Thank you and likewise. My name is Bertha Mullins."

As she walked inside, Bertha mused over the name, Aldrich. An old name. A virtuous name. While bemused by the dinner invitation, Bertha had to focus on the job interview. Earning a living was her main concern. Losing her previous position came without warning. She was stood down without notice. But Bertha had the aptitude and was quietly confident of finding new employment.

Her self-assurance was not misplaced.

The interview went well and was followed by a casual ten-minute chat with the head seamstress. Bertha was taken on as one of the haberdashery's menders. Work was to commence the following Monday. Most pleased with the outcome, Bertha was also grateful to Aldrich for getting her to the interview promptly. She was also glad she had accepted his dinner offer. A fitting acknowledgement for his thoughtful gesture.

Still, there was a slight unease all the same. Bertha knew nothing about him. Not normally someone to accept a dinner invitation from a perfect stranger, there were certain etiquettes a lady should follow, and Bertha had broken them all. Her mother, bless her soul, would not have approved.

Bertha and Aldrich arrived at the eating house at the same time. Aldrich was impressed by Bertha's inclination for punctuality. Unlike many of the local establishments that were overcrowded and reeked of body odour, Aldrich had nominated a cleaner, slightly more expensive eating house. Abigail's fitted the bill. A young woman with a cheerful disposition and an apron around her waist showed them to a booth. It was a good distance from the bar and less noisy so their conversations would not be disturbed.

Bertha thought Aldrich was a curious mix, and soon realised that attempts to elicit more than a few sentences from him at any one time was an exercise in futility. Almost. When Bertha asked about his upbringing, however, Aldrich became more purposeful, as though he needed to get things off his chest.

"So, you are an only child?" Bertha asked.

"I am."

"You left home at a young age?"

"I did. My mother and I didn't get on."

"I see," said Bertha, debating whether to delve further as it was only their first dinner together and possibly their last. "She was terribly strict, I gather."

"More of a tyrant."

"No father?"

"I never knew my father and I doubt my mother knew who he was either."

Understanding Aldrich's meaning, the last comment was unsettling, so Bertha quickly moved on. "And what age did you leave home?"

Aldrich looked at Bertha with an inquiring eye. So many questions. Then again, she had a right to ask, so he said, "I saw my mother for the last time shortly before my fifteenth birthday. One day I walked out the door and did not return."

"Goodness." Bertha was taken aback by Aldrich leaving home at such a young age.

"I have not regretted for one minute leaving when I did. My mother had issues, not least of all her drinking. My younger years were not a happy time." Aldrich was not embarrassed and was not looking for empathy. He was being factual. No more, no less.

Bertha felt the urge to reach out for Aldrich's hand, such was her sympathy for his plight. She did not want to come across as too forward, so resisted, and kept her hands on her lap.

Aldrich very well remembered the last day he saw his mother but the exact circumstances around his departure would not be divulged. He had planned his move for weeks. Aldrich had become quite skilled at stealing food and looking after himself. It was time to branch out on his own. One morning he gathered his meagre belongings into a small bag and walked from his bedroom for the last time. The room, where as a child, he had been visited by his mother's friend.

Molested. Tormented. The faceless woman with the foul breath and the wandering hand.

Hoping to avoid his mother, as he walked from the premises she arrived home, unexpectedly. There was a confrontation and she slapped him across the face and pushed him back inside the doorway. Calling him an ungrateful shit who was lucky to have a bed, Aldrich saw red. He pulled out his pocket knife and after a brief scuffle, he pinned his mother on the kitchen floor, the blade uncomfortably close to her throat. He recalled his spiteful words, lucidly. "You fuckin' bitch, I'll kill you."

Stunned by her son's rage, all she could say was, "Aldrich, no."

It was the first time his mother had looked so scared, her eyes pleading for mercy. Aldrich came so close that day to slicing his mother across the throat. The ecstasy he felt at seeing her squirm and beg for her life. For so long she had had the power but now he had the ascendancy, and his mother was the weaker. She had always been the weaker of the two. Eventually, he got off his mother and put the knife away. The lasting image of her snivelling on the floor was most rewarding. He had wondered in the years since whether he had regretted not stabbing her and the answer was always in the affirmative.

The bitch didn't deserve to live.

For a time, the questions stopped as both Aldrich and Bertha concentrated on the food. For main course they enjoyed steak pudding and potatoes with a gravy sauce. No alcohol passed their lips. Another box ticked as far as Aldrich was concerned, the demon drink was to be shunned. Also encouraging was Bertha's dialect. Not having grown up in the East End, she didn't speak in that dreadful cockney slang, impressing Aldrich immediately.

The arrival of dessert coincided with more questions but none about Aldrich's mother. There was idle chit chat about the East End and Aldrich's job. Both agreed the custard pie was even more enjoyable than the steak pudding. Two hours later and their first dinner together had ended. After taking care of the bill, Aldrich escorted Bertha back to her temporary residence with agreement of another engagement the following week. It was an enjoyable night for both. Aldrich tipped his hat to Bertha and departed.

Over the next month, they saw each other intermittently, usually for lunch or afternoon tea on a weekend. Bertha understood Aldrich was a man of few words, but he was curiously tantalising. Not revealing too much about his background, he had had an unhappy upbringing, Aldrich confirming that his mother had failed him. A mother who drank excessively and who entertained men for work ... and pleasure. Bertha could see the distress it caused Aldrich. He did not need to say much. His words were often obstruse, but the underlying message was undeniably sorrowful, his dark eyes clouding over when he spoke about his childhood.

In the first week of Autumn, Aldrich proposed. There was no getting down on one knee or presenting a ring in a small box. At dinner one night Aldrich just came out and asked and Bertha accepted. He could have been asking Bertha about the weather or commenting on the clothes she was wearing; such was the nonchalant manner in which he proposed. No hesitation on Bertha's part and she accepted on the spot. Mrs Aldrich Eckersley sounded perfectly delightful. Having had only modest contact with men, Bertha was unsure when, and if, another man would enter her life. But being left on the shelf was not something Bertha could possibly accept.

Goodness gracious. No way.

While Bertha was raised Christian, Aldrich had no religion. The idea of a civil marriage did not impress Bertha, but after weeks of argument she reluctantly agreed. Both managed to get time off work for the Friday morning marriage at the register office at Somerset House in Central London. Her parents long passed, it was just the two of them and the marriage registrar, a middle-aged man with greying hair and thick glasses. His high-pitched voice was a distraction, with Bertha having to stifle giggles. A charwoman happily agreed to be a witness as a ten-minute break from her menial cleaning duties appealed to her.

Impatient for the formalities to be over, Aldrich remained detached.

The legal proceedings were over before they had started. No time to take in the little atmosphere there was and the magnitude of the occasion. The registrar congratulated them, Aldrich kissed Bertha on the cheek, and they were done. It wasn't quite the marriage she'd had in mind, but three months shy of her twenty-fourth birthday, married she was. Bertha was tied to a man for life. A man she had known for just six months. A man she loved. Almost. There would be plenty of time to fall in love with Aldrich. All in good time.

There was no honeymoon. They were due back at work on the Monday morning. Soon after the marriage, Aldrich and Bertha settled into a residence in Aldgate, above a shoe shop in Fenchurch Street.

Michael Jenkins had phoned Henry with the name of a hypnotherapist. He could not remember who was going to contact who about Mary Wilson either, but on a whim decided to phone first. She had a practice in Henley Beach, just a stone's throw away from where Henry lived so the location was ideal. Henry and Claire wanted a speedy resolution to the nightmares that had plagued their family, the last few incidents with Harriet of most concern. The nightmares had gone on long enough.

While they had the hypnotherapist's name and location, the bad news was the four-month wait to see her. Like many professions and trades, an acute shortage meant there was a long delay. Absurdly so. Henry and Claire were despondent but had little choice. They had to hang on and hope there would be a cancellation in the interim. Unlike Lucy who had not had a recurrence of her nightmare, Harriet had been troubled by the dreams. Outwardly, she remained stoic, but Henry and Claire knew otherwise. Deep down she was a very frightened girl. The incidents, however, as bad as they were had had one positive outcome: an improved relationship with their daughter.

Eager to read Bertha's journal, Henry had been shut out as Harriet was not keen to give it up. Not just yet. After disclosing its existence at dinner, she had been reading excerpts every day. The more she read, the more captivated she had become with Bertha's life. Never one for history, the readings from her great-great-great-grandmother's diary had gripped her like nothing else she could recall. Even the cute boy bands on YouTube and Spotify couldn't compete.

After moving back and forward over the months of 1888, Harriet had gotten to November of that year and Bertha's mention of their impending journey to Australia. Bertha initially expressing unhappiness with the decision; a decision that ignored her feelings, but then having a change of mind. It was a new beginning that she hoped would strengthen her marriage with Aldrich.

Harriet moved forward to 1889.

Sunday 23 June 1889

'Adelaide is a pleasantly ordered city. Unlike the East End of London and its crowded streets and markets, there is plentiful room to move without bumping into people. The weather is a vast improvement on England and the sky always seems a rich blue. Aldrich has a job working for the quarries while I have a position as a seamstress at a house that has been converted into a dress factory. Our new cottage is coming along beautifully, and the garden is looking more presentable each day. I have planted English roses near the front fence which I must confess have greatly enhanced the entrance to the house. I always wanted roses but living above a shoe shop in London and not having my own garden to tend to made that undertaking impossible. Roses can make a garden. So enchanting! The local flora on the other hand is not so much to my liking but that's a personal opinion and not one, I am certain, that is shared by the local folk. I have ordered a few varieties of English seedlings, namely Silver Birch and Oak, which will arrive on the next ship that is due in two months and in good time for a spring planting. I do hope the trees flourish in this hotter climate. They will require plentiful watering.'

Harriet closed Bertha's journal and slipped it under her pillow. Sleepy, she closed her eyes. An inner warmth enveloped her, Harriet was feeling happier. Bertha's anguished comments about her cheerless life in her earlier writings had been replaced by more inspiring sentiments. The darkness had been replaced by a brightness.

Bertha's life was turning around.

Over consecutive nights Aldrich knocked on Bertha's door. Twice more. That's all it took. Bertha soon fell pregnant. She was over the moon. The baby she had always desired. That was the easy part. The pregnancy itself was not so easy, Bertha suffering from awful morning sickness. The sea sickness on the voyage to Australia had been gruelling, but her pregnancy sickness was sapping her energy. Each morning, she was most unwell and keeping food down was next to impossible. While Aldrich empathised as much as Aldrich could, his brooding ways were often simmering close to the surface. Bertha was too unwell to be bothered with her husband's mood believing he would have to fend for himself in the weeks and months ahead.

Her focus was simple. To look after her physical health and her growing baby.

Each month provided additional challenges, Bertha rising to each in the only way she knew how. With a fierce grit and determination. Still believing a baby would be best for her marriage, Bertha, despite feeling wretchedly ill, approached each day with optimism. Her unborn baby would be healthy. The journal entries continued throughout her pregnancy, though many of the accounts were shortened as each day was much like the previous day. Bertha did not venture past her rose garden and her front gate, and she had to give up her job as a seamstress because of her delicate condition.

The nine months seemed like an eternity.

When the time came for the birth, Aldrich was directed to his bedroom for the duration of the labour, the bossy mid-wife having none of his carry-ons. Bearing seven children herself and having delivered numerous babies, her instincts told her there was no place for a man during the birth. Especially men who were short on compassion and empathy. She put Aldrich in that basket despite only having met him the once. His sour, expressionless face was enough to put her off.

The labour was only three hours, and after months of morning sickness that was a blessing. With the aid of the bossy mid-wife, Bertha's baby was born on the kitchen table without complications. Aldrich was finally let into the kitchen by the grumbling mid-wife, who told him in no uncertain terms that he should stand clear while she cleaned up. An exhausted Bertha was sitting in a chair cradling her baby. While not wanting to hold his new-born immediately, Bertha sensed new-found pride in her husband. A brightness in his eyes had replaced the soulnessness of the past.

Born at ten minutes after midnight, the girl weighed in at five pounds, four ounces. She cried, loudly.

Aldrich had asserted that the girl was to be named Mary-Jane. Bertha had not considered many girl's names as she was confident she'd have a boy. She was wrong. Nonetheless, Bertha was overjoyed the baby was healthy. There would be no arguments over names.

Mary-Jane Eckersley it was. Bertha was euphoric.

Chapter 14

Harriet could hear John crying, but he was nowhere to be found. She searched all the bedrooms and still no John. Was he deliberately hiding from her? Though many months in the past, John may still have been annoyed at her for breaking his dinosaur. The cry was faint, but it was her younger brother. She knew her brother inside out. Every sound he made. Cry. Laugh. Yell. Botty burp.

"John, where are you?"

There was no answer. She repeated the question but still there was nothing.

Harriet would not be discouraged. While John could be very irritating, she loved him, as she loved Lucy. There would be no let up until he was found. Unlike the other boys in this part of the borough with their grubby faces and shabby clothes, John was well dressed. He would stand out in the crowd.

"John, it's Harrie, come to me."

Harriet left the main street and ducked down a lane way. Day was turning to night, but she could still see where she was going. The cobble-stoned laneway could be tricky, and Harriet was handicapped by her high heels. Carefully she trod.

Harriet intensified her pace despite the high heels and the roughly edged path. A cat jumped from a cardboard box in front of her. Harriet squealed and the cat scurried off. She had to find John before nightfall. She rounded a corner and almost collided with several more boxes. Regaining her balance, the sight was confronting.

The cat was mangled. The bloodied head was smashed in. Sickening. Was that the cat she had just seen? Who would do such a thing?

On she walked and soon Harriet was outside a house. She pushed the door open and looked about the small room. A fireplace, several small tables, a chair and a bed. The bed was empty; the mattress was dirty. There were remembrances.

"John, are you in here?"

The memories were becoming clearer. Harriet had been in this room before. The woman who had died in a most horrible manner. The room that was coloured red. The boy was by the fireplace. The same boy Harriet told to play in a sandpit. It was a place where six-year-old boys belonged.

"I'm looking for my baby brother," said Harriet, with some urgency.

The boy's facial features were misty. He did not speak.

Defiantly, Harriet said, "I'm looking for John and I'm not going without him."

The boy pointed above the fireplace. The woman was slouched on another woman's lap. Distressed and grieving the loss of a loved one. Such sadness and anger. The seas could be so unpredictably cruel. No sooner had Harriet spied the two women in the painting than the boy had vanished.

Just like the last time.

A man in a long, dark coat entered the room. The bed was now occupied. A woman was lying, but not moving. Was she asleep or dead? Harriet could not tell. The man reached under his coat and pulled out a knife, the blade glinting in the semi-darkened room. Now she remembered. Harriet knew what was coming. Horrible. She tried to run but her legs were fastened to the floor. Soon, there would be blood. Lots of it. All over the bed and the walls. She had to get out ... and fast.

The stranger kept striking the woman. Unremittingly. Ferociously. Each time the blade came down on the wretch of a woman, the stranger whispered things which Harriet couldn't make out.

The woman was beyond help. Harriet took several tentative steps back toward the fireplace. The hand on her shoulder made her jump. The hand belonged to her father. Her dad's face was reassuring.

"It's going to be okay, darling," said Henry in a soft voice. "No one will hurt you."

Harriet's relief was palpable. She hugged her father. She wasn't about to let go.

Harriet woke. It was morning and John could be heard playing in his room. He was singing one of his favourite nursery rhymes, 'Row, Row, Row Your Boat'. She got out of bed and dressed, remembering every detail of her dream. The stranger she saw in her nightmare and in the bathroom, and the woman being attacked. It was all so vile.

Harriet ran to her parent's room. Without knocking, she entered. They were sitting in bed. "I had another dream and this time I remember everything. The woman and the man who killed her. It was terrible."

Henry said, "I know. I was there Harriet. I saw what you saw. I think we shared the same dream."

Harriet slid under the blankets between her parents. "You reassured me with your hand on my shoulder. I was calmer because you were with me. What the hell?" said Harriet, confused by what had taken place.

"It's all so stuffed up," said Henry, identifying with his daughter's confusion. "It's time we filled you in on a few things, darling. The bedroom in the dream, our dreams, was where a woman named Mary-Jane Kelly died. She rented a small room. She had few possessions, but there was a painting titled The Fisherman's Widow which hung over the fireplace. She was Jack the Ripper's last victim, or so we believe ... so the authorities believe."

Harriet's look was quizzical. "I think I've heard of Jack the Ripper."

"It was a long time ago," said Claire.

Continuing, Henry said, "Mary-Jane's death was particularly wicked. She was ... well, cut up badly. The Ripper was also responsible for four other deaths in London's East End. There were five victims, then the murders stopped."

"How awful," said Harriet. "And he was never caught?"

"No," Claire said, "The murders ended almost as soon as they began, and no one knows why. A mystery to this very day."

Harriet, holding her parent's hands, said, "You once talked about a psychiatrist, but I don't think that will be much use."

"Why do you say that?" said Henry, curiously.

"What's happening to us can't be explained by logic. Let's face it. This is super weird. Bad shit ..." Realising she'd dropped a swearword, Harriet hesitated but her parents didn't comment, so she pressed on. "We were in the same nightmare. Seeing the same things. This is not normal. The woman dying at the hands of that monster."

Henry was temporarily stunned by his thirteen-year-old daughter's explanation. Sometimes Harriet could astound. One minute bawling, uncontrollably, over a netball loss and shoving her sister off a bed; the next, she was providing rational thought to an incomprehensible series of events.

"Harriet could be right, Henry. Perhaps we don't bother with hypnotherapy. Mary what's her name, or anyone for that matter."

"Hypnotherapy? No one's mentioned this before." This was a new one on Harriet. Where did this come from?

"We haven't spoken to you about it yet, but Michael Jenkins believes a hypnotherapist could unlock these dreams. Perhaps there's something in our heads sparking all this rubbish. There's a lengthy wait, so we don't have to decide now whether to see her or not."

Harriet shook her head, frustratingly. The prospect of the nightmares continuing did not thrill, Harriet hoping for an answer. By someone. Somewhere. If a hypnotherapist could help, then so be it. "What do we do?"

"Not sure, sweetheart," said Henry. "We are no closer to understanding this. I know one thing. While the nightmares are disgusting, we don't seem to be in any danger, not physically anyway."

"Seriously!" Claire was astonished. Henry was wrong on this point.

Detecting his partner's cynicism, Henry piped up. "What I meant to say is that no one has been hurt so far. They are dreams." Henry was just trying to lighten the load but, admittedly, the sight of Harriet holding a knife over Freddy was scary shit. Henry and Claire feared poor Freddy was about to cop it. They were clutching at straws. They were clueless as what to do next.

"Oh Henry, I hope you're right. Our family must be safe. All these terrible incidents." Tears welled in Claire's eyes and seeing her mother visibly upset, Harriet was also moved to tears.

Mother and daughter cuddled.

Adelaide
Friday 21 November 1890

'I have not made a journal entry for a few days. The shock of what has befallen our family has caused me much anguish. This is difficult for me to write but write I must. If being a mother to a little one has not been difficult enough, to lose your husband in the most unfortunate of circumstances has been a bitter pill. A policeman knocked on my door last week to tell me that my dear Aldrich had passed. My wailing would have been heard as far away as North Adelaide but I'm not ashamed. It was the awful shock. I could barely hold myself together as the police officer helped me to a chair and explained the circumstances of Aldrich's death. I cried for hours. I am still crying. The events around Aldrich's death are the subject of conjecture. He was apparently knocked to the ground and run over by a horse and carriage as he was crossing King William Street. The carriage driver failed to stop and the several witnesses to the accident have provided police with statements. The only thing that is not in question is Aldrich was killed while crossing the street. His death was instant. His funeral was held yesterday. A small service at the Anglican Church in Halifax Street, St John's, even though Aldrich was not religious, followed by a burial at West Terrace cemetery. A small group attended the service, some of whom I had not met. May God reward their Christian kindness. I will be forever grateful for the comfort they provided at a time of immeasurable grief. I am now left alone to bring up a six-month-old. I dearly love Mary-Jane. Every day that I look upon her tiny face is another day of pure joy. I believe in the short time Aldrich was with her, he was happier and more content. Sadly, he will not see his daughter mature into a young woman. Now it is just a family of two. The months ahead will no doubt be long and difficult and while I have a few savings, I don't know what the future holds. The local minister says he will assist where possible and the parishioners have also expressed their desire to help. As we have never been regular churchgoers, I am genuinely grateful for their kind heartedness. This may well be my last entry. I have not the energy nor the will to write. What was once my favourite pastime has now become an encumbrance. Perhaps, with the passing of time I will again take pen to paper.

Yours Bertha.'

Harriet re-read the last paragraph; her cheeks dampened by tears. She had to look up the meaning of encumbrance on the internet, a word that made her even gloomier. Bertha had been so upbeat after arriving in Australia and now this. Her life was in turmoil. Again. A new baby. The tragedy of her husband's death. What unimaginable grief.

More upsetting for Harriet, Bertha's final entry was 21 November,1890. Not one word more had she written. What had happened to Bertha and Mary-Jane? Did she re-marry? How did her life end?

Harriet had become so attached to Bertha's life, and she had to learn more. But from where?

Harriet had turned the garage upside down in an effort to find out more about Bertha and Aldrich. The trunk had contained the journal, a scarf and an old straw hat with a floral design but nothing else. She had become fixated with her distant relative. Harriet rifled through more boxes but none of the items bore any relevance to the 19th century ... England or Australia. There were Christmas decorations, tools, books, computer cables and clothes worn by Harriet and Lucy when they were toddlers.

"What's up, sweetie?"

"Looking for more stuff on Bertha." On all fours, Harriet had her head buried in another box, tinsel in one hand, a baby bib in the other, when her father turned up.

Any luck?" said Henry, bemused but impressed by his daughter's obstinate pursuit of her great-great-great-grandmother's life story.

"Nah." Disappointingly, Harriet's search had proven fruitless, and she was about to give up when her father appeared from the house.

Henry and Claire were at a loss about how to tackle the dreams but were more concerned for their daughter's mental health. If she was preoccupied with Bertha, then all the better. Anything to distract her from the Ripper killings. "There'd have to be info on when they arrived. I'm guessing. We can always go online and check one of the genealogy sites."

Harriet's face lit up. "Great idea, Dad."

"I'm full of good ideas, darling."

"Yeah, yeah! Don't be big headed." As much as she loved her father, he could be so daggy. Loveable but daggy. "Let's go." Leaping to her feet, Harriet rushed from the garage. "Come on, Dad, no time to rest."

Henry chuckled. "No time to rest. Really!" A quaint idiom uttered by his daughter. Claire was so much in Henry's ear about resting more often that she would surely disagree.

Chapter 15

Henry had chores to do, but Harriet would not leave him alone. For an hour she had followed him around the house. Upstairs. Downstairs. Inside. Outside. Wherever Henry was, Harriet was never far behind. She wore him like a glove.

"Do you really need to be on my tail all day, Harriet?"

"Sorry Dad but I need your help tracking down Bertha's story. The parts I don't know about." Harriet was not at all sorry but given the circumstances believed it was the right answer. She did not want to piss her father off. Not totally and not yet. She needed his help, and besides, their relationship had changed for the better. Now was not the time to damage their newfound friendship.

Finally, Henry caved in. "Okay. Enough now," he said, mildly irritated as he entered the kitchen for the umpteenth time that evening. Knowing his daughter was on a mission, his white flag was at full mast. He was a beaten man. "Give me twenty minutes to finish what I'm doing, and I'll see you in my office."

Harriet's smile was triumphant. "Thanks Dad." Her persistence had paid off. Dying to find out how Bertha had fared in her final years, between the pair of them they may have success. As the saying goes, two heads are better than one. Harriet had searched online but had little to show for her efforts. Excited at what lay ahead, Harriet was seated in her dad's office before the intended time. She was ten minutes early.

"I'm ready."

"So, I see," said Henry, pulling up a chair next to Harriet, and switching on the laptop. Henry typed in the password and the screen came to life. Rather than go to a genealogy website first, Henry began looking at old newspaper articles. It was worth a try. Typing in several key words including Bertha's name, he had to scroll through page-after-page before a collection of stories came up.

One article read: 'The colony of South Australia in its sixth decade still has a relatively modest population. The answer could lie with immigration'. The article went on to talk about the impending recession and tough times ahead for many South Australians.

Henry scrolled down to the next story, as Harriet leant in, almost rubbing against her father's two-day stubble.

"This is interesting."

"What's interesting," said Harriet, hanging on her father's every word.

"The story says ... oh dear!"

"What?"

"Aldrich Eckersley was run over and killed by a horse and carriage in 1890. I sort of remember dad talking about a relative dying in tragic circumstances. I thought he'd drowned at sea." Henry continued to read. "They never found the carriage driver. Hit-and run. And I thought hit and runs were a new phenomenon. Apparently not."

"It was in Bertha's diary ... the death of Aldrich. She talks about a horse and carriage." Harriet was overwhelmed. It was the sadness of reading about the death of Bertha's husband. Poor Bertha! What she must have gone through.

"You never told me, Harriet."

"I only read about it the other night. It made me unhappy. What else is in the story?"

Henry kept scrolling but details were scant. Closing the article, he continued to comb the internet. Scanning two more articles in quick succession, they were deemed irrelevant. Then. "... Hang on. Here's something."

A small story in The Advertiser dated 1917 mentions the forthcoming nuptials of Mary-Jane Eckersley to James Evans, a prominent Adelaide physician. "So, James was my great-great-grandfather's name. Wow," Henry said.

'Mary-Jane, the daughter of the late Aldrich Eckersley and Bertha Eckersley, currently residing at East Terrace and James Evans of Kensington Park are to marry this Saturday at St. Peter's Cathedral in North Adelaide. They will be married by the Rev. T. S. McCarthy. A formal reception will take place after the service at Ayers House in North Terrace. Guests will include Mrs. Eckersley and Mr. and Mrs. Jonathan Evans.'

"Gee looks like Mary-Jane married into money. It would have cost a small fortune for a reception at Ayers House back in the day." Henry was quietly gobsmacked. Mary-Jane, a first-generation Aussie landed on her feet. Big time!

Harriet was about to ask who Ayers House was named after but did not want to be side-tracked. "So, Bertha saw her daughter marry. That's good." Harriet was relieved after learning of the news." Harriet did a quick calculation in her head and said, "Bertha would have been in her late fifties or early sixties by then."

"I guess you're right, darling."

"Any other stories about Bertha, Dad?"

Henry googled a few more pages, let out a sigh, then closed his laptop. "I think we're done for now, Harriet. But we've learnt that Aldrich and Bertha's daughter married a fella called James and that Bertha attended the wedding."

Harriet remembered Bertha's final words in her journal, 'This may well be my last entry. I have not the energy nor the will to write. What was once my favourite pastime has now become an encumbrance.'

Harriet was pleased Bertha had lived long after her husband and seen her daughter marry. Still uncertain what she had been doing in the more than 20 years between Aldrich's death and the wedding of her daughter, Harriet took herself off to bed. Almost satisfied. There was still more to uncover about Bertha. A lot more.

But at least they had made a start.

The winter months went by without much fanfare. Henry was busy at his surgery; the children were at school and Claire, with Freddy constantly by her side, looked after the day-to-day running of the household, as well as upholding her part-time job at Adelaide University lecturing in geosciences. Early spring soon made way for late spring. The Henley Hawks were enjoying another good season, the narrow loss the year before all but forgotten. The coach had told the players to focus on the now and not dwell on the past. It was music to Harriet's ears who was keen to move on. She could not change the score. Like the death of Julius Caesar and the sinking of the Titanic it was etched in history.

So why fret?

With two rounds to go, the Henley Hawks were on top of the ladder, having lost only one match. The two-goal loss mid-season was to the same team, the Glenelg Gazelles, who beat them in the preliminary final. The coach, the team and the parents were trying to keep a lid on it, but expectations were high. Very high. And rising.

Soon to turn fourteen, Harriet was on tenterhooks. Henry and Claire were doing their best to keep Lucy and John from being too annoying around their sister. Many days were spent walking on eggshells. It was the norm rather than the exception. While Harriet's temperament and dealings with the family had significantly improved, when it came to netball nerves, not much had changed.

Counting down the days, the netball season for Henry and Claire could not end soon enough.

Henry had little time to further investigate Bertha's life because of work, much to Harriet's frustration. Harriet was told she had to put more time into her schoolwork which was also a bother, but she understood her parent's motivation. Grudgingly. Harriet could not ignore the love of her family. The chat in her parent's bedroom after she had shared the same nightmare with her father had made a big impact. A game changer!

For the first time, Harriet felt they had treated her as a young adult. And closing in on her fourteenth birthday, she believed she had earnt that right.

After winning their last two minor round games, the Hawks sealed top spot on the ladder. Easily. The Gazelles were second placed, so the two teams were likely to meet in the finals. The Hawks, with Harriet playing the best netball of her career, sailed through their first finals' matches to advance to the grand final. Henley had a week's rest before the final match of the season. Not surprisingly, Glenelg also won through to the grand final setting up a much-anticipated rematch. Or grudge match as Harriet liked to describe it.

Harriet had learnt to hate the Gazelles. As did her teammates. They would take no prisoners on Saturday. She well understood that hate was a strong word, but it was also a motivator. And after the last big loss, Harriet needed to be on song.

Harriet, aware of her amplified anxiety when she played sport, tried to remain calm in the lead up to the big game ... but best laid plans! She fought with the whole household. No person or animal was off-limits. Everyone was too noisy. Everyone was too offensive. Everyone was getting on her nerves. Harriet did not concede for one minute that she may have been the problem child. Even Freddy couldn't take a trick. If he barked, Harriet would growl back, and Freddy would withdraw to his wicker basket.

It was a very long week for the family. They were all feeling the strain. They also understood Harriet's nervousness with the grand final looming.

The night before the grand final Harriet was restless. Edgy about the game, she tossed and turned and at two in the morning went downstairs to have a glass of milk. Anything to settle the nerves. She downed the glass without taking a breath and headed upstairs, passing a sleeping Freddy in the hallway. Dear Freddy! And to think she almost took a knife to him. Shit! She had to rest but the more she thought of sleep the harder it became. She kept tossing and turning. Her mattress was so uncomfortable.

First alienating her family, now Harriet and her bed were not on friendly terms.

Finally, she gave up on sleep. She switched on her bedside lamp and reached under her pillow. Looking over Bertha's diary may help. She turned to a page in 1888 and revisited one of the entries. She read about Bertha's great sadness in London before the happiness of experiencing her daughter's marriage.

With a colossal yawn Harriet was about to close the journal when she saw a small piece of paper sticking out from under the back cover. What's this? She tugged, ever so slightly, but the paper was stuck to the inside. With a little more force the paper came loose. Harriet unfolded the paper, delicately, and to her delight realised it was from Bertha. The foolscap paper was not dated but it was Bertha's handwriting.

What was this? Harriet was elated. Smothering another yawn, she read:

'Rather than commit at once, I thought I would write a separate piece and consider it carefully before adding it to the journal. The war has ended but what a terrible toll it has taken. The British empire and the Commonwealth countries, including Australia and New Zealand have suffered devastating casualties. It was a just war, I firmly believe, but the loss of so many young soldiers has been horrendous. My heart grieves for the fathers and mothers who will not be welcoming home their sons. Their inconceivable grief is my grief too. They say it was the war to end all wars. Dear Lord, I pray that to be the truth. The world cannot take another tragedy, certainly not the likes of what we have witnessed these past few years. While the battlefields of Europe have been awash with our young blood, the only light in my life has been the marriage of Mary-Jane to James. Both are clearly in love, and I wish them every blessing for their future happiness. Fortunately for Mary-Jane, James was rejected for service because of a gammy leg. He was born with a condition that made him unfit for service. James is studying to be a doctor, but it is his untold devotion to Mary-Jane that I find most pleasing. He is an exceptional young man.'

Harriet tried to read the next sentence, but the ink was smudged, some of the words difficult to read. That line she skipped.

'My garden continues to flourish. The seedlings brought out from England all those years ago are now well established and the trees have grown well above my head. I suppose after twenty-five-years, or there-abouts, they would have matured into very large trees.

The climate here with the year-round sun has been very good to them. I do love my garden so.'

There was another sentence that was difficult to decipher so Harriet skipped to the bottom of the page.

'In the years since Aldrich has passed, I have learnt things about my late husband which, quite frankly, have disturbed me deeply. There was a darker side to Aldrich, much darker than I could have known or ever imagined. It may explain why he was so obsessed about leaving London. The decision to pack up without consulting me was inexplicable and hurtful. However, as I was his wife, I believed my spousal duty was to support my husband and determined I was to carry out that responsibility. I am reluctant to officially write this in my journal as I find it difficult to believe and to understand. It has been brought to my attention, distressingly, that Aldrich was a ...'

"You got to be kidding!" yelled Harriet.

Damn. The word was blotted. The last two letters looked like an e and an r. What are you saying Bertha? There had to be more. She turned the page over, but it was blank. Not another word was written.

Bloody hell.

What on earth did Bertha mean? Caught between Bertha's letter and the urgent need for sleep to be best prepared for the match and the biggest game of the year, Harriet was in a quandary.

How could she possibly sleep after learning about Aldrich's darker side?

But how dark was he? Where was Bertha going with her writing?

Suddenly, the grand final against the Glenelg Gazelles had lost some of its impetus. Harriet's mind was in sprint mode about Aldrich. Sleep would not come easily. After watching several music videos on her smartphone, eventually she nodded off with the words, 'Aldrich had a dark side', reverberating in her head.

Chapter 16

The next morning Harriet was still in a tizz after reading Bertha's reference about her husband's darker side. What had he done? That the family had a possible criminal in their ranks was a shock. Unbelievable, crazy shit! Her parents had always championed their respective families. Not that dad had much idea about his family background, but mum at least always spoke glowingly of her family. If there was a crook, more than likely it came from dad's side. The mad medics! Harriet giggled. And if her great-great-great-grandfather was a villain, talk about upsetting the applecart! Harriet was in a state of panicky excitement.

The big game. Bertha's admission. Holy hell!

Changing into her netball gear, Harriet was dashing here, there, everywhere, and picking up and throwing her clothes around the bedroom. At will. She had over-slept and only a thump on her door by her father roused her. Already eight-thirty, the match was scheduled for ten that morning and the players were expected to arrive at least an hour before the start. She couldn't be late. Not today of all days.

After finding matching white socks she raced down the stairs. The car was in the driveway, the engine running, when Harriet fled the house with one shoe on, the other in her hand. She leapt in the back almost squashing John, pushing him across to the middle seat as she buckled up.

Playing with his dinosaur, John did not even complain about the rough treatment handed out by his sister. Rex was about to attack Freddy, so John had bigger things on his mind. Oblivious to John's intentions that he was about to be ambushed, Freddy was already napping on Lucy's lap while Claire was in front with Henry behind the wheel.

Harriet had made up her mind. There would be no mention of Bertha's note. Now was not the time to tell the others. This was her day. Her day to shine. For the Henley Hawks to shine. The premiership and boasting honours for the next twelve months were up for grabs. Harriet believed they would bury the Glenelg Gazelles and avenge last year's defeat. Then Harriet, once-and-for-all, could wipe the blemish from her memory and the agonising last minute when she failed the team ... and herself.

Unlike previous seasons, Harriet was happy to have the family supporting her, loudly or otherwise. The coach had revved the players up before the match, explaining why they deserved to be in the grand final. Being the best team all season and finishing minor premier, it was no fluke they had found themselves in the big dance.

While still early in the day the temperature was climbing steadily, many of the girls perspiring before taking to the court. It was not uncommon for November to be hot, especially if a north wind was blowing from the desert. The game likely would be a grind, the coach stressed, the warm conditions playing a pivotal role. So, it was important for the girls to start well.

Henry and Claire, along with John and Lucy, found a spot on an incline that gently sloped down to the playing area. Their view was uninterrupted. They had taken up positions with dozens of other Hawk's supporters while the Glenelg fans had congregated on the other side of the court. Lucy and John had ice creams while Henry and Claire were sipping their lattes. They exchanged pleasantries with the families they knew from previous games, but the chatter was brief. Everyone was focused on the big game. And everyone was on edge.

"Why are Glenelg called the Gazellies?" said John.

John's question like most of his questions came out of the blue. Knowing better than to laugh at her younger brother's question, Lucy shot her father a teasing eye. Her father didn't bite. While he may have found the question funny, Lucy couldn't detect a smile as he quickly bent down to pat Freddy who was lying at his feet on the grass. Lucy and Harriet sometimes couldn't help but poke fun at John, earning the ire of their parents.

The innocence. The inquisitiveness. Claire marvelled at her son's curiosity. "Well, sweetheart. The word is actually Gazelle and it's an African antelope."

"Oh."

Claire could tell her son had yet to understand what a Gazelle was, so she said, "I presume they chose Gazelle because it's a fast animal. Sporting clubs like to pick the names of animals they think match what they want to be. Netball is a fast game and Gazelle sort of rhymes with Glenelg. They both start with G."

Claire knew her answer had failed to make headway as John was hungrily licking his ice cream. The subject was quickly forgotten as the game was about to begin. In truth, Glenelg had been known as the Gazelles for many years and Claire had no idea why they had that name, but her guess was as good as any. Besides, she was talking to her six-year-old son and any explanation would do. For now.

About to add to the discussion, Henry was left hanging as the bell went. The game was underway.

The first half went goal-for-goal, neither team gaining an advantage. Much to Henry and Claire's delight, Harriet in her usual goal defence position was playing strongly, her opponent having little influence on the game. The same opponent who made the winning throw up forward that resulted in a goal for the Gazelles and the preliminary final win a year earlier. Harriet gave her no breathing space. She was virtually standing on her toes. That was her coach's advice, and she was unwavering in her efforts to carry out that task.

By three-quarter time, the Hawks were one goal in front. A bruising affair, girls from both teams had bloodied knees and elbows after being slung unceremoniously to the hard asphalt surface. Several girls were also hobbling. Noticeably. A case of the walking wounded. For the uninitiated and those seeing the game for the first time, news that it was a non-contact sport would've come as a shock. It was a final after all. As the coach said there could only be one victor. It was a war of attrition. The coach's final instructions were followed by an inspiring battle cry, the girls yelling, 'Hawks Fly Forever, Hawks Fly Forever.'

As the bell rang to signal the start of the last quarter, Claire and Henry gave Harriet a thumbs up. Seeing the gesture, she smiled. The crowd was on its toes for the last, decisive fifteen minutes. Henry and Claire were nervous nellies and could hardly look at one another. Lucy, understanding the importance of the game, had her eyes proudly on her sister, while also holding John's hand who was more interested in rescuing the last of the vanilla ice cream that was dripping onto his shirt.

Unlike the last big loss, Henry and Claire were confident their daughter had matured enough to accept defeat if that was to be the outcome. The family had been through hell over the past year, and they had grown closer, Harriet accepting that her parents were not the kill joys she had long imagined. The nightmares had united them in a way none of them could ever have envisaged. While Harriet was confident of victory, her parents were more guarded, appreciating the opposition's recent success and ability to win the tight games.

But Harriet and her teammates were chasing victory. Anything less was unacceptable.

Claire could not watch the agonising final moments. With five minutes remaining on the clock, she bent down and stroked Freddy. The suspense was too much. No such reaction from Henry, Lucy and John who were spellbound. The ball zipped from one end of the court to the other. Ridiculously fast. Spectators were treated to a worthy climax. The grand final was living up to expectations.

The game was not for the faint of heart.

Claire was carried along with all the whoops and whoas. Henry was under strict instructions not to divulge a score unless the Hawks were in front by three goals or more with less than a minute to play.

"Come on. That's ridiculous," shouted Henry.

Claire could tell Henry was unimpressed with an umpiring decision, but she still refused to look. Her eyes were fixed on Freddy. The excruciating seconds seemed like minutes, but Claire soon received a tap on the shoulder.

"It's okay, Claire. I think they're home." Counting down the last thirty seconds, a confident Henry was calling the game. "Henley are going to win."

Claire stood, her gaze shifting to the scoreboard: 52 to 48. The Henley Hawks were leading. The bell went. Mayhem broke out. With Harriet and her teammates hugging and high fiving one another, their supporters stormed the court. There were scenes of sheer exhilaration and amongst the beaming faces there were tears and laughs. A year of pain had ended with victory over the arch enemy, the Glenelg Gazelles, with Marcie who played goal attack, singling out Harriet for a hug. Their embrace was heart-felt and long-lasting.

After Harriet had congratulated her teammates and was toasted for her own performance by her coach, Harriet ran to the sidelines and to her over-joyed family. The same family she had accused of handicapping her for so long. Unappreciative and holding her back. But not now. She wanted them to share in her moment. Mum and dad were the first to be hugged. Then it was Lucy and John's turn. She pulled them close and tentacled her arms around them. All three pirouetted deliriously for some seconds. Lucy and John could not stop laughing and Harriet could not have been happier. She did not want the moment to end. Every single second had to be treasured. Harriet had the best family in the world.

The revelries had begun. The family would soon head home to celebrate Harriet's accomplishment with lunch on the patio.

The call to Henry was unexpected. Mary Wilson had had a cancellation. Initially, he wasn't sure whether to accept the hypnotherapy appointment for the following Friday morning. He would be late for work, and his patients would have to be rescheduled. He sought Claire's opinion. Both procrastinated. There had been no nightmares for many months and Henry and Claire were increasingly confident the worst was behind them.

But there was always the 'what if' question hanging over their heads like a bad smell. After much toing and froing, they agreed Henry and Harriet should see the hypnotherapist. Just in case. While Lucy had also experienced a nightmare, they believed she was too young. She had also been free of bad dreams since the episode in the Flinders Ranges.

Mary Wilson had come well credentialed; Michael Jenkins having known her since their primary school years. A friendship thirty years in the making. Operating from her suburban home at Henley Beach, except for a small sign on the front gate that read: 'Mary Wilson Hypnotherapy', no one would have been the wiser that it was a business. It was the new normal. The pandemic had forced many people to run their businesses from home. Mary Wilson had joined the ranks. Happily!

Claire drove Henry and Harriet to the appointment. More than capable of taking himself, for some odd reason Henry was apprehensive. Nerves had developed during the night and an offer by Claire to drive them was willingly accepted. Was it the thought of being hypnotised and quizzed by a fellow medical professional? Henry had no idea, but it was a restlessness that he had never experienced before.

Harriet, on the other hand, was looking forward to the appointment. She had heard about hypnotism and found the idea intriguing. She had also seen a few hypnotists on television and thought their magic was cool. Making contestants bark like dogs and meow like cats was hilarious. After the traumas of recent years, she had no hint what to expect but she'd go with an open mind. And who could argue against a morning off school. Claire dropped the pair off, arranging to come back in an hour after she had been clothes shopping. Bargain hunting, she told Henry, of a therapeutic nature. She had to fill in the time, somehow.

Henry laughed.

Henry was expecting to be met by a receptionist as he and Harriet knocked on the door, but as he was about to learn, Mary Wilson was no one-trick pony. With a cheery smile as the door opened, she told them that as well as running each one-hour session, she oversaw all the appointments and even made the tea and coffee. Mary was nothing like Henry had imagined, not that he had had much time to picture her.

Approaching middle age with similar strawberry blonde hair to Claire, Lucy and John, she was tall with olive skin. But it was her thick caterpillar eyebrows that attracted Henry's attention. Fascinatingly, they moved up and down like a fast-moving drawbridge when she spoke. Henry had to force himself to keep eye contact and not be distracted by her eyebrows. He hoped against hope that Harriet wouldn't be amused by her eyebrows and start to giggle. Once Harriet got the giggles, she found it hard to compose herself. And like father like daughter, if Harriet lost it, Henry knew he wouldn't be able to contain himself.

After a brief introduction, Harriet and Henry were shown into a room with three cushioned chairs positioned in triangle formation. The curtains were partly drawn allowing in some filtered light from the outside.

Smiling, Mary said, "Nice to meet you both. I'm not sure what you know about hypnotism, but I'll give you an idea how it works. Then, if you have questions, fire away!"

Harriet and Henry nodded as they sat.

"Has Michael told you about our issue?" Henry said, hesitantly.

"Only that he had a friend I may be able to help and that you both have had bad dreams of a similar nature."

Henry said, "Our problems began well over a year ago …"

"Hold that thought. I'll let you know what I do first, but my aim is that you come away feeling relaxed, and your overall mental well-being is much improved. The idea is to focus your attention but at no stage will you be asleep. You will be listening to my voice; my suggestions only, and you will be conscious at all times."

"No pig and chicken noises?" Harriet chuckled, determined to make the session fun for her and her father.

Henry sniggered.

Laughing, Mary Wilson said, "No, nothing like that Harriet, but I like your quirky thinking."

"Quirky. That's one way to describe Harriet," Henry added.

Henry was pleased to learn there would be no watch swinging back and forth past his nose. Not that he expected hypnotherapy to be practised like that in the 21st century. His problem was he had seen too many movies featuring gullible characters, dazzled by a watch, their heads pivoting from side-to-side.

Soon it was Henry's turn to speak. The explanation began with Lucy's dream in the Flinders Ranges before he detailed the worst of the nightmares ... those that he and Harriet had suffered. Seeing Freddy in bits and pieces and then stabbing Lucy was diabolical. The recurring nightmare about Mary-Jane Kelly was also spoken about. There was no mention of his earlier concerns about him being Jack the Ripper. No point now as his train of thought had moved on. For the better.

The dreams were so vivid, Henry asserted. "Like we were there."

Mary Wilson had hardly flinched until Henry's bombshell disclosure that he believed they may have been witnessing the London murders in 1888. Her expression altered. While thinking Henry's claim was wide of the mark, she was nonetheless dismayed. The manner of the woman's death was terribly sad. Real or otherwise. Were they repressing long-held memories of someone else's death? A loved one? Was there some awful secret the family had buried for decades?

"Hopefully, I can unlock some of your memories and see what's been causing these nightmares," said Mary Wilson. "I don't usually take two people in the one session, but because you're related and have had similar experiences, I believe it's appropriate."

Father and daughter exchanged smiles.

Mary Wilson suggested Henry and Harriet move their chairs closer and hold hands. Without hesitation, Harriet reached for her father's hand. Mary Wilson began, her words mellifluous. "Let's start, shall we? Concentrate on my voice and my voice only ..."

Chapter 17
Spitalfields
Friday 9 November 1888

Mary-Jane Kelly lay on her bed, her eyes gradually closing. It had been a long night drinking with friends. Her mind was splintering. So many things to consider. Some good and some bad. There was the twenty-nine shillings in back rent she owed, catching up with Lizzie for a drink and her intention to return to Limerick. She'd had enough of London and its dirt; its crime; its sleaze. She should never have moved to England. It was a mistake she now regretted. Longing to go back to Ireland, Mary-Jane was determined to make it happen before the spring.

Nine years had passed since her marriage. Only sixteen at the time, no amount of persuasion from friends would prevent her from marrying her beau. She was so much in love and talk of being too young was poppycock. While a few of her friends had tried valiantly to talk her out of marriage, Mary-Jane had her Da and Mam's blessing and that's all that mattered. Mary-Jane believed that her parents wanted all their children, except the eldest who was destined for a religious life, to be married off at an early age. They wanted them off their hands. Feeding so many kids was a financial strain.

But losing her husband at such an early age was devastating. She would never have left Ireland if her husband was still alive. Bugger him! Why didn't he listen to her about the dangers of his job. Spending hours underground in a coal mine in Ballingarry was dangerous. Everyone knew it. So many miners had died in the past. The risk wasn't worth the money.

Mary-Jane often said to her husband, "I want to have a family with you. But if you want a short life then continue working in the mining industry but you'll leave me a widow."

Intuitive words that proved accurate. Tragically.

Before she was married it was mass every Sunday and on Holy Days of Obligation. Da and Mam insisted the family never miss a Sunday service, unless someone was sick. Even after her marriage, she attended mass each Sunday. Often, she went alone as her husband was working in the mines. Most prayers were asking God to keep her husband safe. But the death of her spouse changed everything. God had ignored her prayers, so Mary-Jane now ignored God.

The anger intensified to a point where Mary-Jane knew she had to get out of Ireland. Start afresh in a new place. Her travels took her to London, but it was expensive. Food and rentals did not come cheaply. She tried several menial jobs, but the pay was poor. Nothing satisfied. If she was to eke out a reasonable living, she had to change tact. Be bolder and more daring. Take on the world!

She had written to her Da and Mam just the once since arriving in London. As her parents were illiterate, the letter was sent to her older sister who could read and write. The contents of the letter could be shared between her parents and her seven brothers and two sisters. It was filled with pleasantries about the things to see and do in London, the people she had met and how she missed her family. Terribly. The guilt about her work life stayed with her constantly.

Mary-Jane briefly mentioned that she had picked up employment at a match factory and part-time work as a domestic cleaner. The latter was true, the former not so. She hated the lies but had to reassure her parents that they need not worry. She was in good spirits and living the good life in a big city. She signed her letter with 'Love you all. Always. Mary-Jane.'

Mary-Jane had been told since childhood that sex outside marriage was a mortal sin. But if she were to survive, selling her body would be her saviour. Like most things in life, it didn't come easily but after a few months and an increasing clientele, many of them regulars, many of them considerate, the work became effortless. Like learning to ride, once you got on the bicycle the pedalling was easy. Mary-Jane told herself that she wasn't a bad person, and she would not be punished for her impiety. If God existed, she would be forgiven.

That's what she kept telling herself. Each day.

Mary-Jane had been told she was attractive, not that she saw herself as pretty, but the compliments were welcome all the same. Her blonde hair and blue eyes had been eye-catching features from an early age. For now, there would be more nights luring men for their satisfaction, but once she was back in Ireland with her people that would end. She would get a respectable job and renew old acquaintances. And have that large family she had always wanted. But find a new husband first, she would.

The one person she'd regret leaving behind would be Lizzie, her neighbour and friend. Over the years they had had many heart-to-hearts. Lizzie was a good friend and confidant who accepted Mary-Jane for who she was without judgement. Many nights they had laughed their problems away over several pints and solved the world's problems. They were the best nights when Mary-Jane's work was pushed to back of mind; no thoughts about intoxicated clients and doing tricks. There had been the odd close call with boozed customers who argued over the cost, but nothing Mary-Jane couldn't handle. Knowing she could be feisty; the feistiness had helped her in sticky situations.

Mary-Jane felt the need, often, to warn Lizzie against being on the streets. Once, she had told her, "Whatever you do, don't you do wrong and turn out as I have." It would bring her nothing but trouble. And Mary-Jane, shrewd as she was, understood all kinds of trouble.

Being youthful, she had ample time to turn her life around. No way would she finish her days like her older associates and friends, the women she had gotten to know around the East End. Many were much older than her and still peddling their wares. But time was their enemy. Middle-aged, their use-by-date was pending. They were going nowhere because they had nowhere to go. They were women with no future.

Damn her husband for leaving her to fend for herself in an unkind, uncaring world that she loathed.

Her life could have been so different if only he had heeded her advice. No use lamenting and feeling sorry for herself now. Too much water had flowed under that bridge. So, back to Limerick by the spring. That was the plan. It was a good plan. Her early grief and loss and her lifestyle choices would not define her. She would rebuild and be happy.

As Mary-Jane dozed, dreaming about the next phase of her life, she was faintly aware of the bedroom door opening. If not a workmate looking to stay over, then more likely Lizzie or one of the tenants from upstairs. Mary-Jane often invited associates to stay if they had no permanent lodgings. Her door was never locked. A kind heart and a munificent welcome for those in need. The winter nights could be cold and unforgiving.

There were more happy thoughts about Ireland. Not long now until she saw her Da and Mam.

Henry had a firm grip on Harriet's hand. "This way, sweetheart."

As they crept through the shadowed room, Harriet wasn't sure this was a good move. The room was dank with a poor odour and the muskiness was an irritation to her nose. "Where are we going, Dad?"

"I'm looking for a way out."

"I'm scared. Can we leave now?"

"I'm trying, believe me."

They came to a door that was slightly ajar. Henry pushed and it opened. Easily.

"This way, Harriet." Henry led his daughter into the next room. Instant recognition. The anguished women in the painting and the woman lying on the bed. A single candle was burning in a jar on a small bedside table.

"Oh Dad, not this again. We have to leave. Now!" Harriet's heart was pounding, strongly. She did not want to see the poor woman's horrible death. Not again. Like the last time they were irresistibly drawn to the bed. Forbidden from leaving. "We're back in this room. We need to get out," said Harriet, anxiously.

"Yes, we do, Harriet."

Harriet had witnessed a terrible crime in this room. She had been trapped before, unable to move her legs, with the room closing in on her from all angles. The woman was murmuring in her sleep.

"Dad!" Harriet was freaking out. "He'll be back to kill her. We must leave now!"

Henry had no answers. He had to protect his daughter, but he was immobile.

Henry and Harriet were forced back to the fireplace and under the painting of the Fisherman's Widow. There was tapping outside the door. Both had heard the noise before. The stranger walked in, cane in hand, and approached the woman on the bed. He placed his hat on the table next to the burning candle.

For the first time Henry noticed the black feather in the man's hat. A strange addition to male headwear, Henry determined. Harriet had also described a feather in the stranger's hat when she had the vision in the bathroom.

Henry and Harriet were helpless. They knew what was coming. Henry shielded his daughter as the first cut slashed the woman's throat. Like the time before and the time before, the dozing woman did not react, blood gushing from the deep wound below her chin. No mercy was shown. The next assault was aimed at her breast. The hacking was fast and furious, each penetrating deeper into her soft tissue, the dirty mattress turning red.

Life was being viciously extracted from the woman with every savage blow.

The stranger enjoyed what he was doing. So gratifying. So invigorating. His job was far from done and the whore would be unrecognisable once he had finished. He tore off her clothes, threw them into the hearth and with the candle set them alight. Her frayed clothing was quick to burn. The stranger then approached the woman.

The fire had breathed new light into the darkened room. He now had a clearer view of what remained of her face. She was younger than the others. She had blue eyes, but the blood had turned her fine blonde hair red. There was a tear in one of his eyes. He hovered over the body for some seconds as if wondering what next to do. She was already dead so there was no going back. Anyway, his mother was to blame. His arm raised; the stabbing began again. Feverishly. Hardly an inch of her pulverised body was spared by the blade.

"I'll do what I want to do. No one can tell me not to," the stranger snarled.

Mesmerised by the brutality and in a bid to stop the onslaught, Henry reached for the killer's arm. His efforts were in vain. Henry was uncertain how long they had been in the room. The frenzy continued unabated. By the time the killer was done the woman had no face. No face at all. The stranger wiped the knife on the blanket to remove the blood stains. He collected his hat and faced the fireplace and Henry and Harriet. His expression was blank.

Disgusted, Henry and Harriet felt his presence pass through them. They were bystanders to a crime that had taken place more than a century past. Henry glimpsed the killer's face clearly for the first time. Someone he knew. Somewhere from his past. The black hat; the dark eyes; the moustache; the cane.

The stranger reached the door and said, angrily, "They'll never tell me again. I'm in control. Not them."

This time Henry heard him. "You've killed innocent women. You're a monster." Henry meant to keep the comment to himself but instinctively raised his voice due to the horrific nature of the attack.

The stranger pounced. Henry was in his sights. Stepping back in fright, Harriet screamed. Henry raised an arm to protect himself from the knife, but he was slow to act. The blade was forced deep into his ribs. Henry stumbled. Fearing Harriet was next, he placed his body between her and the killer to shield her. But the assailant fled out the door. Where Henry expected pain and blood there was none. Just like the earlier dreams he hadn't been harmed physically.

Harriet, relieved, placed a supportive hand on her father's arm as they tried to work out what had taken place.

Henry held Harriet. "Thank God. You're safe ..."

"And you, Dad."

Standing between Henry and Harriet, Mary Wilson's face had turned a pukey, pallid colour. Even her overactive eyebrows were in a holding pattern. After looking from Henry to Harriet and then back at Henry, she finally said, "Are you two, okay? That was bloody hectic!"

Henry answered first. "I'm fine; you, Harrie?"

"Okay. But seeing the woman's death again ... I feel sick," said Harriet, disconsolately and wiping away a tear.

"I'm not sure what happened. One minute you were listening to me, then you both appeared to be in a kind of trance. I couldn't get through to you. It was like you were in another place."

"We were somewhere else," said Harriet. "In the room where the woman was murdered all those years ago."

"Mary-Jane Kelly was one of the Ripper's victims," Henry added. "She was butchered. Her death has been repeating in our dreams. In our visions."

Becoming slightly panic-stricken, Mary Wilson was not in control of her two patients. No matter what she said, neither responded to her suggestions. They were a world away! That had never happened before, but she would not admit that to her two clients.

"All good. All good," Mary Wilson repeated, uncertainly. The words were more for her own comfort than her clients. "You're back in the land of the living."

Usually unflappable, Mary Wilson had been ruffled by the incident. Badly. Details about Henry and Harriet's ordeal could wait. They had been incommunicado for close to half an hour and her next client would soon arrive. Never had she not been in control of one of her sessions.

Why didn't they hear her? Were they back in late 19th century England as Henry had suggested? No way but ... Because of the eeriness of what unfolded, she suggested a second appointment in a month's time.

Henry and Harriet left without committing to another session.

Most days around lunchtime and between clients, Mary Wilson brewed a cup of tea, but after the morning session her hankering was for something stronger. Much stronger. Still shaken by the experience, two generous nips of brandy were added to her tea. A nerve settler that she hoped would make a difference. Only two more clients and she could call it a day.

Dinner that night was on the patio. Neither Henry nor Claire was in the mood to cook so they ordered fish and chips. There were no dissenters as fish and chips were a family favourite. Just one of many family favourites. The delivery included hamburgers with the lot, dim sims, potato cakes and oodles of hot chips. Taking it in turns, each of the children secretly passed Freddy a chip. Such was the generosity of the children who loved nothing more than sharing with Freddy, Henry and Claire were staggered their dog was not a very plump ball of fluff. They figured the daily walks were a help in keeping his weight down.

No great surprise that the hypnotherapy session dominated discussion while they ate, albeit with sensitivity while Lucy and John were at the table. Mary Wilson had a taste of what the family had been living with for over a year. The ugly events surrounding Mary-Jane Kelly's brutal murder had been on constant playback in their dreams.

John and Lucy were the first to finish their meal. They were in a rush to watch a movie about a brave dog who rescues a family during a flood. The dog happened to look like Freddy which made the film even more appealing. As he passed Harriet, John gave her a hug. "Love you, Harrie."

John's action surprised everyone, not least of all, Harriet. "Love you too, John."

Harriet kissed her brother on the cheek before he and Lucy hurried inside.

"The whole thing was sickening but awesome," said Harriet, who was still strained from the hypnotherapy session but tickled pink by her baby brother's show of emotion. "One minute Mary was talking to us and then we were back in the room seeing the murder."

"Awesome is one word I wouldn't use to describe it. Not sure I want to go through that again." Henry was ambivalent about the events of that morning and dubious of the worth of another hypnotherapy session. "Mary labelled it 'bloody hectic'. I can think of more descriptive words, especially since the bastard attacked me. I shouldn't have called him a monster but then it was a dream ... I think!"

"Dream or no dream he was a monster, darling," Claire said, caringly.

"I'm still at a loss to understand how he heard me and why he reacted if it was a dream or a vision. The murder happened over a hundred years ago. Were we really in Mary-Jane's room or not?"

Said Harriet, sheepishly, "Maybe all this has something to do with Bertha's journal. I meant to tell you ... the night before the netball final I found a piece of paper in her diary. She claimed Aldrich had a darker side. A much darker side."

Stunned, Claire said, "Did she say what specifically?"

"All she said was that it had come to her attention he was a ... well, the note finished there. I couldn't make out the last word."

"My great-great-grandfather had a darker side. Seriously! He couldn't have been all bad. Aldrich's grandson was a doctor. As was his son. As was my father. As am I."

"Don't take it personally, Henry. There's good and bad in everyone." Claire could sense her husband's frustration and was keen the discussion did not become an all-out attack on Henry's ancestors.

Sceptical, Henry was unsure how to take his daughter's news, but the revelation unlocked a memory. "There was something else. As the killer left Mary-Jane's room, he said, 'They'll never tell me again. I'm in control. Not them.' I may have misheard but I don't think so."

Harriet concurred. "Yes. I heard him say that."

"What's all that about?" said Claire, contemptuously.

Henry shrugged. "No idea but I got a good look at him. In the past his face had been blurry, but this time he stared straight through us. There was something about him."

"Like what, Dad?" said Harriet.

"Not sure but it's time to go back online. Something I need to check."

"Awesome." Harriet was over the moon. There were things she still needed to know about Bertha. "Come on, Dad."

"For goodness sake, Harrie, give your father a break."

"It's fine, Claire. I love her enthusiasm."

Claire smiled. "I'm glad everyone got through this. You two have more work to do so I'll clean up."

Henry and Harriet got up from the table. "Thank you, darling," said Henry.

"All good. Off you go."

Chuckling, Henry turned to Harriet and out of the blue said, "And what about those eyebrows?"

Harriet laughed. "They were spectacular."

"I could have watched them all day!"

"Seriously, Dad. Let's go."

Henry and Harriet laughed as they walked inside the house. Claire was left to ponder what they were talking about. Eyebrows! Whose eyebrows and what was so funny? She was about to ask but the moment had passed. The joke could stay between father and daughter.

"I've got a hunch, but I won't say until I have a clearer idea," said Henry, logging on to his computer.

"Really, Dad." Harriet was less pleased with hunches being kept from her. Information should be shared. Then again, Harriet had kept from the family Bertha's comment about her husband having a dark side. She justified her silence because of the importance of the netball final. There were other things on her mind.

"I just want to be sure, sweetie. Work with me on this."

Henry spent the next few minutes surfing different websites, listing the sailing ships that had berthed at Port Adelaide in the late 19th century. The sites gave extensive details, with arrival dates, names of passengers, ship manifests and the cargo onboard.

Henry scrolled down a list of ships. The Murray, Rodney, Yatala, St Vincent, Torrens, Coonatto, Orient and The Goolwa.

After getting Bertha's journal from her bedroom, Harriet was checking entries from early 1889 to confirm their arrival date from England. After turning over several pages she found what she was looking for. "Here it is, 16 February 1889. Bertha said they took seventy-eight days to get here. They travelled on a ship called the Torrens."

Henry did a few calculations. "Excellent. That means they left England on or around 30 November 1888." Henry soon found details about the Torrens and its captain. The clipper was built in England in 1875 and scrapped in Italy about thirty-five years later ... goodness. Joseph Conrad, the famed writer, served as chief officer on two of the return voyages from Adelaide to Plymouth. How interesting!"

"Don't know him." Harriet puzzled over the name, Conrad, wondering whether she should have known about him.

"No reason why you would have at your age. He wrote Lord Jim, among other novels and short stories. I read Lord Jim in high school. A bloody good book set on the high seas ..." Henry was about to correct his swear word but let it pass. There were far worse expletives and Harriet would only think him a bigger fool for expressing regret. How prudish could he be?

Harriet was clueless, so Henry kept skimming. "Henry Robert Angel was the captain. His son, Falkland Angel, took command in 1896. There you go!"

"Falkland! God, they had weird names back then." For someone who hated history as much as he professed, Harriet was amused by her father's fascination with the Torrens. He could be such a dag!

"On one voyage she lost her mast when she hit an iceberg near the Crozet Islands and made it to Adelaide with a badly damaged bow."

"Crozet Islands?" said Harriet.

"No idea where they are if that's what you're asking."

"Not really." Harriet was over the history lesson, so in a supercilious voice, she said, "Back to Bertha and Aldrich!"

On another website Henry discovered a newspaper article from The Evening Journal describing the arrival of more settlers from Britain. It had a February dateline which was hard to read. "I might have something here, Harrie. The story talks about the Torrens and its arrival at Port Adelaide. There are photos too."

Henry zoomed in on an image of one couple and the caption underneath. "Jackpot!" Henry almost fell off his chair when he saw the names. "Aldrich and Bertha Eckersley. Bloody hell! It's your great-great-great-grandparents."

Standing, Harriet moved closer to the computer screen. "Can you enlarge the photo?"

Henry played with the image but there was little he could do to enhance it. Their faces were difficult to make out, but Aldrich was a few inches taller than his wife. He was wearing a hat and a coat and was holding a long cane. Fairly typical of that era. Bertha also wore a hat and had a shawl around her shoulders. They didn't seem to be smiling but no one did in those days. Something to do with the camera's slow aperture. Or perhaps smiling for the camera wasn't the done thing.

"They'd have felt the heat in those clothes if it was a typical summer's day. Poor buggers," said Henry, showing empathy for their plight. "The caption reads: Mr. and Mrs. Aldrich Eckersley, formerly of Aldgate, London, arrived on the Torrens yesterday seeking their fortune in the new colony and the promise of a better life."

Henry perused the article but there was no further mention of his long-dead relatives. "Sorry, Harrie, no more on this site. Time for a break. My eyes are stinging."

Also having had enough for one day, Harriet was content to call time on their father-daughter quest. Working with her dad on such an exciting project gave her a new perspective. The boring, demanding father figure had given way to a more understanding parent.

She didn't see it coming but her father had become her friend.

Henry was about to close his laptop when he said, "You know. The dates are curious. They left London just weeks after the last of the known Ripper murders in 1888. And Aldrich had a hat and a cane like the bloke in my dreams."

"Our dreams, Dad," said Harriet, quick to correct her father.

"Our dreams," agreed Henry.

Harriet made for the door, then said, "What are you saying, Dad? That your great-great-grandfather was Jack the Ripper."

"Yeah, nah. I'm not sure what I'm getting at. It's bad enough that he had a darker side. Whatever that means."

"I guess we'll never know, will we?" said Harriet.

Harriet was soon back in her bedroom. As she flopped onto her bed, Bertha's words were front of mind. 'Aldrich had a dark side.' Still curious, Harriet wondered what Bertha was getting at.

Long after his daughter had left his office and responding to her comment about his relative possibly being the Ripper, Henry said to himself, "I guess not, Harrie. We'll never know."

That his great-great-grandfather could have been the infamous Jack the Ripper did not sit well with Henry. It was one thing for Bertha to talk about Aldrich's dark side, but was he a killer? There had been speculation that the murders were committed by someone with a knowledge of human anatomy. Coming from a long line of doctors the incongruity of it all was not lost on

Henry. Some of the surgeons at the time rejected the killer had any anatomical expertise, instead suggesting the victims were hacked to death by a crazy man. Aldrich, as far as Henry knew, had no medical know-how but he could have been crazy!

Recalling the words of the killer, "I'm in control. Not them." What did he mean and what was he thinking?

Henry stood as Freddy, tail wagging madly, scurried down the hallway. "Time for a walk, Freddy. Let's find your leash. I need to clear my head."

As he logged off from his computer, Henry considered what he had seen. There was a slight resemblance between the man in the newspaper article and the person in his dreams. Certainly, the clothes were similar. If only the photo had been better quality. If he was a betting man, Henry would have wagered that they were one and the same.

Henry, however, was not a betting man.

Unlocking the front gate with a leashed Freddy champing at the bit, Henry stopped. The killer's words, 'I'm in control. Not them,' playing on his mind. What did he mean? The killer relished every cruel stab. They were all prostitutes and he clearly hated prostitutes. Perhaps he was after women of a particular height or hair colour.

"Sorry Freddy, the walk will have to wait." Henry went back to his office and logged on to his computer, revisiting the details of each of the five murders: Mary Ann Nichols, Annie Chapman, Elizabeth Stride, Catherine Eddowes and Mary-Jane Kelly.

After an hour he had made little progress. A piece of the puzzle was missing. The women had had different upbringings. By all accounts they didn't know one another, but a few may have crossed paths because of their work and the same areas they frequented. Not entirely implausible. Henry opened the saved files on each of the women. Keeping in mind the information collated by the police was well over a century old and some of the details were vague at best, he went over their particulars again. Their backgrounds. Their friends. Where they died. The last person who reportedly saw them alive.

And there it was. Staring at him. The missing piece of the puzzle. The victim's ages when they died.

Mary Anne Nichols was aged forty-three; Annie Chapman was forty-seven; Elizabeth Stride was forty-four and Catherine Eddowes was forty-six. The odd one out was Mary-Jane Kelly who at twenty-five was the youngest victim ... by a country mile.

Was the killer targeting women in their forties? If so, how did he muck up with Mary-Jane, his last kill? The room was very dark according to the police report. He may have followed her back to her premises at a distance after seeing her prostitute herself. Then came the killer's frenzied attack in her room and perhaps the realisation when it was too late that she was much younger.

Perhaps Jack the Ripper had an ounce of humanity, after all. Not an ounce but a smidgeon. Henry soon dismissed that thought as silly because anyone who could do that to another human being had no humanity. None at all.

Logging off, Freddy having gone to sleep at his feet, Henry felt a release ... of sorts. Much of it was mere speculation. None of it would hold up in a court of law but it was noteworthy all the same.

Twelve months later

It was late afternoon, but Harriet had to touch base with her father. As the door to her father's office was closed, she thought better than barging in. There was a time she wouldn't have given two hoots about bursting in unannounced. Her father's feelings were inconsequential. But the newer, more mature version of Harriet was a different person. So much had changed.

Harriet knocked once. "Just me."

Through the closed door, Henry said, "Come in, Harrie. I'm glad you're here. I've got something to tell you."

Henry was pleased to see his daughter; their relationship having gone from strength-to-strength after a wobbly start to her teenage years. At her lowest ebb, the nightmares had not helped but no one had experienced one for over twelve months. They had ended, suddenly. Just like the murders in 1888. Everyone was grateful.

"What's up, daddio?"

Henry shuffled a wad of papers around his desk, before turning his attention to the computer. "Pull up a chair. I think I found something in regard to Mary-Jane Kelly's death. I did another genealogy search and came up with this."

Henry opened to a page and began to scroll down the text. "Guess work on my part but I found the birth date of Aldrich's mother. Freda Eckersley, nee Johnson was born in London on the ninth of November 1842."

The date meant nothing to Harriet.

Excitedly, Henry added, "It was the date of Mary-Jane's murder. A coincidence or what?"

"You said at the time Mary-Jane was the youngest victim and the others were much older," said Harriet.

"That's right. I'm wondering if that date was deliberately selected by Aldrich if he was the killer because it was his mother's birth date. I can't find out any information on Freda but perhaps their relationship was fraught. Something about her; something in his background may have turned him into a sadistic killer."

"I like it, Dad."

"Thanks Harrie. I thought you'd like to know." Henry was proud of his detective work, even if he was completely wrong. But the possibility that his great-great-grandfather may have been a ruthless predator still pained him.

"Speaking of theories, I have one too," said Harriet, almost forgetting why she had wanted to see her father. "When I found Bertha's journal in the garage, it was about the same time you had your first nightmare. I saw the date of your appointment with Michael Jenkins on the wall calendar and mum's diary confirmed it."

"Really!"

"Yes. Your nightmare occurred about a week or two weeks before your first appointment. I remember the timing of the diary because it was a Saturday, and I was pissed about babysitting Lucy and John ... and having to pass up the movie with Milly."

"And shoving Lucy off the bed and making her cry." Henry couldn't let the opportunity pass to rib his daughter. Jokily.

"I've tried to forget about that," said Harriet, ruefully. Breaking John's T-rex was also not forgotten. Two incidents that she was hardly proud of but thankful they were many months in the past. Still, the reminiscences were embarrassing.

"Just stirring, sweetheart. The appointment! That's good, Harrie. Even if you're right, we don't know why the dreams stopped."

"And probably never will. I'll never get the image out of my mind of that poor woman being attacked."

Henry took his daughter's hand. "Mum and I are so proud of the way you handled yourself throughout that period. It was hard enough for us to deal with but you ... a thirteen-year-old. You know we think you're amazing, but I'll say it again ... you're amazing."

"Thanks, Dad. But I haven't always been amazing. I was a pain for a long time. Not just with Lucy and John but with you and mum."

Treating her brother and sister badly was one thing, but Harriet was also sorry for how she had spoken to her parents. She had taken out her frustrations on her family and at times had been dismissive and outright rude. There was no excuse, but she had felt worthless, especially after the loss in the first netball final. There were so many things she hadn't liked about herself, her caramel brown hair chief amongst them. But that had changed. Harriet had more self-confidence, and she was more forgiving of herself and of others. She also accepted her caramel brown hair as it set her apart from her mother and siblings. In a nice way. She was unique in her family.

Pushing her guilt aside, Harriet said, "One thing I've never understood. Why didn't mum have any nightmares?"

"Good question. If Aldrich was the Ripper, we are his direct descendants. Your mother isn't blood related. But that's just a wild guess." Henry paused. "Your poor mother has lived through the dreadful experiences too. She may not have had the nightmares, but she was there to comfort us. And hear us all scream! I can't say she's had a great time."

Harriet was convinced that her great-great-great-grandfather committed the murders. Why else did she and her father have the nightmares? Discovering Bertha's journal had played a part in unleashing something sinister. Melodramatic? Maybe. But only after reading the diary did the family's problems begin. For Henry, Harriet and the family.

"I know you're probably not across British history, but they were tough old days." Henry considered his words carefully. His voice was gentle. "There were so many destitute people, especially in the big cities like London. Making a living wasn't easy and some had to resort to prostitution."

Harriet studied her father's face. She thought he was about to cry.

"Except for Mary-Jane, the murdered women were mothers. I'm guessing they had families who loved them: brothers, sisters, aunts and uncles. These women were not bad people. They were just in the wrong place at the wrong time."

Thrown by her father's sudden outpouring of emotion, Harriet said, "I've never judged them."

"I know, Harrie. I just wanted to say they were worthy of a good life but missed out. They drew the short straw. Sorry if that came across badly. I needed to say out loud what I was thinking."

Harriet kissed her father on the cheek. "I can see why your patients love you."

Another hour passed with father and daughter chatting. There were moments of laughter interspersed with moments of sadness, as they discussed the Ripper's victims and the horrors each were subjected to before they died.

The death of Mary-Jane was particularly galling. Her life had been harsh.

Married at a young age; losing her husband after a short marriage; leaving her beloved Ireland for work; resorting to prostitution to survive; and dying the cruellest of deaths. All by the age of twenty-five.

She had hardly lived.

What could possess someone to do such terrible things? As a doctor, Henry spent his days helping people with their medical issues and encouraging healthy lifestyle choices. That some people could treat life so cheaply was inconceivable. Totally at odds with his principles.

If there was a God, Henry and Harriet agreed; Mary-Jane Kelly, Annie Chapman, Mary-Ann Nichols, Elizabeth Stride and Catherine Eddowes deserved a special place in Heaven to make up for their miserable lives and their dreadful endings on earth.

The travesty was that justice was never served as no one was ever held to account for their murders.

Just for a minute and allowing a touch of smugness, Henry and Harriet accepted that their theories about the Ripper had merit. But as much of it was guesswork and the people were long gone, they understood their assumptions could never be substantiated. A shame but it was not the worst thing!

Father and daughter were on the same page. There was more to life. Much more. The love of their family was right up there.

Chapter 18

East Terrace Adelaide

1902

It was too early for visitors. Faithful to the hour, the grandfather clock in the hallway had yet to chime eight times. Bertha wasn't expecting any callers on a Sunday. But there it was, a soft knock, followed by a louder knock. The brief interval between knocks gave Bertha little time to reach the front door. The impatience of some people! As she left the loungeroom, she could hear Mary-Jane playing in the back garden with Fifi.

The brown Cocker Spaniel had been Mary-Jane's pride and joy since her eighth birthday, and four years on they were inseparable. Bertha advised her daughter to play outside early morning and in the evening when the sun was not at its strongest. With her fair skin, Mary-Jane had to be careful not to burn. Such a contrast to her father, Bertha often wondered who in her family was of a similar pale complexion.

Who could possibly be calling? She didn't want to be accused of snooping so resisted the temptation to peer through the curtains. That would be rude. Opening the door, Bertha was met by a short man in a dark suit who was rocking from side-to-side, uneasily. The man had greying hair and was holding a small satchel.

"May I help you?" Bertha asked, politely.

"My apologies madam for visiting at such an early hour and on the Sabbath, but I come with a most important despatch. You are Mrs Aldrich Eckersley I trust. My name is Ross Harkley from the law firm Harkley and Barkley. I'm one of the firm's solicitors and owners."

Bertha's eyes widened owl-like, wondering what on earth the man was talking about. Harkley and Barkley sounded like a three-ring circus. She supressed a smile and not forgetting her manners, she said, "Would you like to come in?"

"Thank you, madam. I shan't be long."

Bertha directed the man to the loungeroom and offered him a chair by the window, but he declined, gratefully. He opened his satchel and pulled out an envelope. His hand was shaking slightly as he passed the envelope to her.

"What is this?" said Bertha.

"I must apologise again." The man took a deep breath before resuming. "We at Harkley and Barkley pride ourselves on our professionalism, our attentiveness to detail and our loyalty to our clients ... above all, our clients come first. Unfortunately, in this instance we have fallen short. This should have been delivered to you about twelve years ago, but it was misplaced. Somehow."

Bertha was speechless.

"Perhaps if you open the letter, things will become clearer. It's part of your late husband's last will and testament."

Finding voice, Bertha said, "But I received his will after he passed."

"Yes, but the letter was also meant for you. It must have slipped between two filing cabinets at our office and was only recently found covered in dust. Fortuitously, the letter is undamaged so the contents should be in reasonable condition." Feeling the need to apologise again, Mr Harkley said, "Most embarrassing. Poor state of affairs."

Bertha opened the letter. Inside were two handwritten pages signed by Aldrich and a newspaper cutting.

Mr Harkley braced himself for a tongue lashing. It was to be expected and would've been justified. But none was forthcoming. Uncertain if he was still fated for admonishment, Mrs Eckersley began to read the letter as if he should be apprised of the contents.

"You don't need to read the letter while I'm here, Mrs Eckersley. My job is done. The letter has been delivered." Mr Harkley, not waiting for a rebuke and searching for a speedy exit, made for the front door, Bertha waving the letter about, a few feet behind.

"Again, my sincere apologies for this interruption on a Sunday. This should never have happened. I hope your late husband's letter brings you comfort and that you haven't been disadvantaged by its delayed arrival. Have a pleasant day, won't you?"

Bertha closed the door as the lawyer from Harkley and Barkley scarpered out the front gate and down East Terrace. She had never seen a man in a suit so fleet of foot. The sight almost made her laugh, but her thoughts soon returned to the letter in hand. Delayed arrival! Was Mr Harkley joking? Twelve years could be classified as more than a delayed arrival. Still, the poor man showed contrition and was very much embarrassed by what had occurred. To front up as he did in person was deserving of kudos.

Bertha returned to the loungeroom and remained standing. She couldn't remember a time Aldrich had written a letter. To her or anyone else. While his verbal skills were modest, at best, his writing proficiency was non-existent. Or so she thought. Then again, while they were married for a decade or thereabouts, Aldrich was somewhat of a surprise packet. Bertha would first read the letter that was undated:

"Dear Bertha, if you are reading my letter then my time has come. I trust you will read with an open mind. I can't say my life has been rewarding but meeting you was the one good thing that happened to me. I repeat, you were the one good thing in my life. I understand I was not the easiest of husbands and there were many times when you wanted more from me, but I did not, or could not, deliver. For that I am sorry. I don't believe in God, and I don't believe I will suffer in Hell for my misdeeds, but I do feel an explanation for my behaviour is warranted.'

Misdeeds? Bertha paused before reading on.

'I grew up with a drunk of a mother who earnt her living by performing immoral acts and I was ill-treated by one of her friends from an early age. I told you about my mother, but the latter may come as a shock. Without going into details, my youthful years were not without regret and misfortune. These experiences damaged me; damaged me more than I realised. Indeed, my transgressions gave me great satisfaction and pleasure. I took revenge on the twisted, worthless souls who were spreading their filth and disease amongst others, people like you and me. My mother died in her forties, so I was determined to do harm to others of her breed and age.'

Was this someone's idea of a silly joke? The letter made no sense. 'Do harm to others of her breed and age.' Feeling sick in her stomach, Bertha laboured on.

'I was in a rage on that last night. The sanctuary of being in her room and not being disturbed was an opportunity I could not ignore. Once I began, I could not stop. It was like that with all the women. I hated not being in control. I had to control them, just as I was controlled by others at a young age. The last incident caused such an outcry, I assumed it was only a matter of time before I was caught, hence the decision to leave England. I also believed that a change of scenery may be good for me.'

Bertha was still struggling with the letter's contents. What had Aldrich done? He was not being specific, and his sentences were cryptic.

'I do not expect forgiveness from you or anyone. Indeed, this is not a letter seeking forgiveness. I understand that many will view my crimes as monstrous and unforgivable. It is up to you whether you keep the details to yourself or divulge the contents of this letter which can be regarded as an admission of guilt. It is your choice. Aldrich.'

Bertha read the letter several times, agonising over certain words, and trying to draw a fit and proper conclusion. Had Aldrich lost his marbles in his final months? Was all this just twaddle? Though twelve years had passed since his death, he was better in the short time they had spent in Australia. The move had been good for him as he had suggested in his letter. He even agreed to start a family. Then he died and that was that.

Accompanying the letter was a newspaper article from the South Australian Advertiser dated Saturday December 22, 1888. The article had been crudely cut out. The headline read: 'The Seventh Whitechapel Murder'.

'During the early hours of the morning of Friday, November 9, another murder of a most revolting and fiendish character took place in Spitalfields ...'

Knowing about the murders in London's East End, Bertha did not care to read the entire article. Was this what her late husband was telling her from the grave? That he was the killer! Why include a newspaper article on the East End murders? Bertha sank into a chair. It was too much to take in. Feeling poorly, she pulled a handkerchief from her sleeve and lightly dabbed her forehead. It had to be a mistake. Bertha did not want to believe any of it.

The marriage to Aldrich had had its fair share of challenges and her life had been far from plain sailing. But her misgivings were few. Bertha had never re-married. There had been a few suitors; men of means and new to the colony who had shown an interest, but Bertha was not inclined to remarry. And certainly not for money. Apathy for a time had set in after Aldrich's death, but she had managed to keep her head above water with the money she earnt stitching garments. Bertha decided she did not need another man in her life. An about-face, she would admit, to the dread she felt at an early age of being left on the shelf. Now middle aged, she would enjoy a modest life with her darling daughter.

About to stand and make herself a cup of tea, the contents of the letter whirling around in her head, a breathless and red-faced Mary-Jane, Fifi lapping at her heels, bounded into the loungeroom. Mary-Jane slumped into a chair, Fifi then jumping onto her lap.

"Having fun, dear," said Bertha, composing herself.

"Very much so, Mother. Fifi loves playing chasey, but I need to rest now."

"You do that, Mary-Jane. There's a good girl. I'll make you breakfast shortly."

The love of an adoring mother was laid bare as Bertha gazed upon her daughter, the troubling contents of the letter receding. Her daughter was the great love in her life. The child she always desired. Mary-Jane did not have Aldrich's brooding, dark eyes. Her rich, blue eyes were always smiling at the world.

"I had a bad dream last night, Mother."

"Darling, that's not good. What about?"

"I was standing on a corner waving goodbye to people, and they were crying. They were sad to see me go! Their tears were real."

"Dreams are so whimsical. No rhyme or reason. Just our thoughts tumbling around in our heads." Mary-Jane had never spoken about her dreams before, so the admission surprised, but Bertha never tired of her daughter's empathetic virtues. The world could be cruel so the longer she held onto the innocence and simplicity of life, the better.

"There was a man tapping a stick or something on the footpath. He had mean eyes and was hurting people. A woman was screaming for help. It was so horrid, Mother."

Bertha said, "Be assured Mary-Jane; it was only a dream. You will have forgotten about it by lunchtime."

"It was as though I was there." Mary-Jane put Fifi on the ground and stood.

"I must insist you forget about the dream, Mary-Jane," said Bertha, whose voice was now elevated. "You'll be fine. Dreams are not real. They can't hurt you."

Displeased by her mother's unfavourable reaction, Mary-Jane politely said, "If you say so, Mother."

"I do say so. Breakfast will be ready soon, so best you clean up. There's a good girl!"

Mary-Jane, with Fifi following, left the room.

Bertha was unimpressed. There would be none of this gobbledygook in her house. After the morning visit with the man from Harkley and Barkley and reading the letter from Aldrich, she had had her fill of ridiculous conversation for one day. Reckless talk about dreams? A man with a cane hurting people. Mary-Jane's dream would soon be forgotten.

Recalling Aldrich's demands at the time, Bertha was happy they had made the long journey to Australia. He said they would be leaving England at the end of the month and Bertha had to pack the trunks. Aldrich would sell off the furniture, including the desk she so loved. Initially outraged, as Bertha soaked her feet in the cold seas at Plymouth before their departure on the Torrens, few doubts remained. Though the long ocean voyage was burdensome, the new country had provided exciting opportunities.

Hopefully, Mary-Jane would have the same chances. With the economy picking up after a long depression, the outlook was looking rosier. While Australia was still gripped by drought, the government said the worst of the economic slump was over. By the time her daughter had finished her schooling in a few years, predictions were for better times.

The solicitor's document still in her hand, Bertha scrunched the letter. Mary-Jane would not be privy to its contents. Not ever. Bertha would not burden her daughter with unmitigated drivel that belonged in a fiction novel. Aldrich was dead so his complicated life would remain buried with Bertha.

Always.

Chapter 19

Adelaide 1932

James Evans was the first to hear his son cry. Not for the first time had he ventured to his son's bedroom after hearing him scream. The early morning visits were occurring with regular monotony. As James entered his son's bedroom, Sylvester was sitting up and rubbing his reddening eyes.

"Father, I had another dream," said Sylvester, wiping away tears. "I'm sorry for waking you."

"You're getting too old for this," said James tenderly. "Little children have bad dreams. You're not a child anymore."

"I know, Father. I can't help it."

Mary-Jane joined her husband and her son. "What's this? Another nightmare, Sylvester? What are we going to do about you? Your scream was so loud it woke me up."

"Sorry, Mother. It was the same man with the same angry eyes. He was trying to hurt me."

"How many times have we told you about dreams. There is no rhyme or reason for them. Just a jumble of thoughts in our heads. They are meaningless." Mary-Jane remembered her mother talking to her about dreams when she was a child. Also troubled by nightmares, she was told in no uncertain terms by her mother to get over it. Life was too short to concern herself with silly dreams, her mother would say.

Mary-Jane saw the damp patch on the mattress. "And you've wet your bed again. Your father is right when he says you're not a child anymore. You'll be out working before too long, so the bed wetting needs to stop."

"I feel like I'm there on the street with this man. He scares me so much. His eyes are dark and …"

"That's enough, Sylvester," said Mary-Jane irritably. "No more talk about dreams. "I'll put a towel down for now and the mattress can be dried in the morning."

"Sorry, Mother." Sylvester felt embarrassed but the man in his dreams was out to get him. Talk of the stranger made his parents cross, but he didn't know what to do. The constant tapping in his dreams was just as frightening. The noise played on his brain, even during his waking hours. While he loved his parents and would do his best not to disappoint them, his fears were genuine. Why weren't they listening to him?

Their only child was a bright boy, and James and Mary-Jane were hopeful that his problems would go away as he matured. James was more patient with his son's issues and wasn't sure his wife was handling it as best as she could. Married for twelve years, James had learnt to live with her single-mindedness, particularly on issues relating to family.

Back in their bedroom, James said, "You don't think we should take him to see someone?"

"You're a doctor, James. Who would you suggest?"

"I don't believe it's a medical issue. But I know that at his age he shouldn't be wetting his bed."

"The situation will sort itself out. You wait and see! Sylvester will manage, just like my mother, bless her, who had to cope as a widow for many years. Life can be tough, unfair, and demanding. We all bear crosses in our lives."

"Your mother was a kindly soul. Not that I knew her for that long before she died," said James.

"She was kind but there was a steeliness about her. She did not suffer fools gladly."

While Mary-Jane dearly loved her mother, her fierce determination could be intimidating. Bertha had been gone a dozen years after falling victim to the Spanish flu. Her mother wasn't forthcoming about all aspects of her life, but she had told Mary-Jane that growing up in London had not been a picnic. Jobs were not always readily obtainable. The population was considerable. Squalor and disease were widespread. Then there was the decision to move to Australia, a country on the other side of the world. A place that Aldrich and Bertha knew little about. But it was a decision that neither she nor Mary-Jane's father had regretted.

Her father's tragic death when Mary-Jane was a baby had affected her mother, deeply, but Mary-Jane always thought there was more to the story. Her mother would go quiet when Mary-Jane brought up her father's early life in England. Mary-Jane believed her mother was hiding things, but she did not know what exactly. It was infuriating. She would change the topic or excuse herself by saying there were chores to be done.

There was an exception.

Her mother would gladly recount the day she met her father for the first time when he showed her the way to the haberdashery. With pride she would vaunt his graciousness, describing how he escorted her to her job interview and dismissing her protestations that she would go alone. Then there was the dinner at Abigail's where they enjoyed steak pudding and custard pie. Her mother's eyes would light up every time she related their first date. She would also regale stories of the long voyage to Australia and the terrible seas sickness that she suffered, and the heat and the flies that greeted them upon their arrival.

But the stories her mother imparted were few. There were gaping holes in her father's life that had never been filled. And they never would be. Her mother's sudden death shortly after the war put paid to that. Mary-Jane's regret was that in her younger years she didn't question her mother more searchingly about her father. Her mother may have confided in her. It was a missed opportunity.

Mary-Jane was not without empathy for Sylvester's situation, recalling her own nightmares as a child. It was so long ago. She was about twelve when they began. But the nightmares had gone away. Eventually. Hers had been a happy childhood. Memories of playing with Fifi, her Cocker Spaniel in the back garden and taking her for walks, always made her smile. Fifi had provided great companionship for Mary-Jane during her younger years. Not having any brothers or sisters, she had long wanted a dog and her mother granted her wish when she was eight years old.

That was it! A dog could be the answer to Sylvester's nightmares. Why hadn't she thought about a dog earlier? Mary-Jane would discuss her idea with James in the morning. She closed her eyes, content with what she had considered as a possible solution. As a child who experienced nightmares, before going to bed she would repeat three or four times, 'Tonight I will only have happy dreams.' Mary-Jane was determined to instill in her son that same positive thought.

Sylvester would soon be a man. About to turn thirteen, indulging Sylvester and his nightmares would be futile. They needed to be ignored for his sake. That was Mary-Jane's firm conviction. That way he would be strong. That way the family would be strong.

The last thing Mary-Jane wanted was for the dreams to take on a life of their own. For heaven's sake, no.

Henry was satisfied. Exceedingly so. He had spent a Saturday afternoon checking the main city cemeteries on the internet including Enfield, Smithfield Memorial and Centennial Park. Finally, he found that his great-great-grandfather, Aldrich Eckersley, was buried at West Terrace Cemetery. The distance between his residence in East Terrace and the cemetery was under three kilometres, so it made sense his final resting place was West Terrace. While pleased with his work, Henry wondered why he hadn't thought of that at the start. It would have saved him time.

Henry had managed to find Aldrich's grave site. The family had expressed an interest in seeing the plot, especially Harriet who had read Bertha's diaries with a shrewdness and maturity beyond her years. All agreed the family would visit the cemetery the following Sunday afternoon. Henry and Claire were not sure it was totally aboveboard, but the children insisted that Freddy also come along. The children would never hear of Freddy being left alone at home.

The weekend could not come around quick enough. It was all Harriet, Lucy and John could talk about each night at dinner. None of them had visited a cemetery before, only adding to the intrigue and excitement. On arrival at the cemetery, Henry took a map from a stand outside the main office that was unattended and searched for the quickest route to his relative's burial place.

After a quick scan of the map and resembling a nineteenth century explorer on an outback expedition, Henry set off confidently with his family in tow. Ten minutes later and after trekking down one gravelly path after another, they came across a sign saying, 'Section R'.

"We're almost there, guys," said Henry, his excitement rising as he scanned the map for a second time. "Just need to find plot number 88."

"I can't wait." Harriet could not believe she was so excited about seeing a headstone. Ghoulish. Until the nightmares and the killing of Mary-Jane Kelly her interest was zippo.

Dawdling well behind the family on the path, Lucy was flicking stones with her shoe while Harriet kept her father company up front. Claire had John's hand who in turn was holding Freddy by the leash. Claire didn't want John to be spooked by the cemetery, but he had shown little inclination for fear. Henry and Claire had gone to great lengths to explain that cemeteries were a place of love. A place where people rested after they died. More appealing to John was the ice cream he had been promised after the cemetery visit. He had told everyone that he would have a chocolate ice cream in a double cone.

After traversing more paths, Henry verified their position on the map. Eureka! They were in the right spot. Henry checked several grave sites and soon found a headstone that was tilting and crumbling. A jungle of weeds had taken over the plot. Henry got down on his haunches and cleared the weeds from the top half of the headstone. He tried to read the inscription but more than a century in the open had weathered the granite slab. "I think I've found the plot. I can make out the word Aldrich, but the surname is hard to read."

"I can't imagine there'd be too many Aldrich's around here," said Claire. She recalled the hysterics around the kitchen table when Harriet revealed the existence of Bertha's diary and her marriage to Aldrich. The family was so happy that night. Claire could not remember a time when everyone had laughed so hard and for so long. What did Harriet say again? Something like Aldrich had an arse of a name. Rather disrespectful but funny all the same.

Squatting, Harriet joined her father at the headstone. "You're right, Dad. It says Aldrich and I can make out the date 1890. I'm sure that was the date in Bertha's diary. The year her husband died."

"That sounds pretty conclusive to me." Claire didn't believe there was a need for more evidence. The name and date were proof enough. While not easily frightened, Claire did not want to spend more time than necessary around gravesites.

Looking as proud as Punch, Henry took out his smartphone and began snapping photos of the headstone and the old engraving. For someone who had never been interested in his family's history, he surprised himself by tracking down his great-great-grandfather's resting place. And he was now taking photos. Wonders never ceased.

"This is your history, Dad."

"And your history too, Harrie," Henry responded, with an air of smugness.

"And mine too," said John, not wanting to miss out, but in the dark as to what history his family were talking about.

"Definitely your history John … and yours to Lucy," Claire added.

Lucy continued to kick pebbles along the path. Talk of the family's history was of no interest to Lucy either. What little curiosity she had previously shown had evaporated as soon as they entered the cemetery. Claire did not want to pour cold water on the family outing, but the gravesite of a long lost relative with a dubious past was nothing she would celebrate. However, despite her misgivings she felt the need to support Henry and Harriet.

"Okay, who wants an ice-cream?" There was no need to hang around any longer than necessary, Claire knowing she'd get an immediate reaction. And sure enough, the mention of ice cream and all three children grinned. John, such was his excitement, began to jump up and down on the spot.

"We've seen what we came to see. Mum's right, time to go." Sensing his family's impatience, Henry agreed it was time to leave. Cemeteries could provide only so much entertainment. Not that cemeteries were meant to be entertaining. While Henry was not particularly religious and not one to dwell on those who had gone before him, he well understood cemeteries were reverential places where people could grieve the loss of a loved one.

"That's a little weird," said Henry, as he eyed the headstone one last time.

"What's that?" Harriet asked.

"There's no mention of Bertha on the headstone and she's not buried next to Aldrich either."

"I wonder why they aren't side-by-side .... being husband and wife and all." Claire did think it strange but was not about to push the point as she was eager to move the family on.

"Very good question Claire but there's a lot about my forebears that doesn't make sense."

With Henry leading the pack, they started back along the pebbled path toward the main gate. Lucy was dragging her heels at the rear and still kicking stones when she stopped. Abruptly. John had tired of minding Freddy, so Claire now had hold of the leash. A few magpies could be heard on a low-lying branch of a nearby gum tree, their melodic warbling soothing to the ear. But it wasn't the sound of the magpies that startled her.

It was something else.

Without alerting the others Lucy made her way back to the gravesite. The noise was familiar. Weird. Exciting. Someone was tapping. Lucy looked around but she was alone. The sound grew louder. The vibration of the tapping noise was irresistible, and Lucy was drawn closer to the headstone.

Lucy's head was now centimeters from the slab. She read the name on the headstone. Aldrich. It was the name her family had joked about at the dinner table. Harriet had called it an arse of a name. They laughed so much their tummies hurt. Lucy knelt and cleared more weeds from around the headstone. Large clumps were easy to pull after recent rain.

Lucy flinched, startled by the hand on her shoulder.

After Freddy had barked, Claire noticed her daughter was missing. She doubled back and was surprised to find Lucy at Aldrich's grave because minutes earlier she had shown no interest.

"Come on darling," said Claire, gently. "It's time to leave."

Momentarily dazed, Lucy was slow to reply. "… Sorry mum. I heard something, and I …"

"That's okay but the others are waiting for us at the main gate. What did you hear?"

"Tapping." Lucy pointed at the gravesite. "Here, where dad and Harrie were. I remembered the sound from somewhere else and it frightened me."

"What have we got here?" Bending down, Claire took a second look at the headstone that moments before was infested by weeds. Near the base of the memorial there was an etching of a top hat and a cane. An unusual tribute on someone's headstone, she mused. People do the darndest things when their loved ones passed. Why on earth would you put a hat and a cane on a headstone?

Though she couldn't hear a thing it was now Claire's turn to be spooked.

She recalled Henry and Harriet's description of the killer and his top hat and cane in their visions. Claire was also reminded of the Flinders Ranges holiday and Lucy's nightmare about the woman with no face. She was silently horrified. Without further conversation, she roughly seized Lucy's hand and briskly marched her away, Freddy scampering obediently behind. Claire's eyes were fixed on the path ahead. She dared not to look back.

Lucy was also told that under no circumstances should she look back.

Les Saunders closed the door to his eighth-floor office in the city. Popular with his colleagues, his door was usually open, but his mood was less than cheerful. A restless night had not helped but more to the point, he wanted to savour his first coffee of the day and enjoy at least ten minutes' solitude before the usual mad rush began. And sure enough, most days he could bank on a mad rush!

Long having an interest in all things crime, suspicious deaths were a fascination so after several years as a junior cop on the beat, he applied to join the homicide squad. He passed the entrance exam with flying colours and quickly rose through the ranks of the South Australia homicide squad. In a matter of eight years, he became one of the highest-ranking detectives in the police squad.

Early on his knack for discerning fact from fiction in even the most complex cases caught the attention of his superiors. When he was not investigating murders and spending long hours on the job, his leisure hours were devoted to television crime shows. It was a pastime passion he shared with his police officer partner of fifteen years.

After logging onto his computer and taking another sip of his latte, he saw the notepad on his desk. On it was scribbled: "East Terrace update emailed to you … makes for interesting reading."

It wasn't long before he found the message from the chief forensic pathologist amongst a multitude of emails in his inbox. He opened the file and began to read. It was a preliminary report on a set of bones that had been uncovered at a location in East Terrace in the city several weeks earlier. More than one set of bones as it turned out. Four skulls had been uncovered during the excavation for a new townhouse complex. Saunders attended the scene, but initial excitement gave way to disappointment as the bones were thought to be of Aboriginal origin and from a period before European settlement.

But as Saunders read further into the document his interest began to spike. The report stated that while only four skulls were found, there were ten femur bones. That meant five skeletons in total. There was evidence of damage to two of the hyoid bones with deep indentations present, possibly caused by a sharp instrument such as a knife. The forensic pathologist determined at least two of the victims were possibly murdered.

Saunders did some initial research after the discovery of the bones. Investigating the city's property records, he found a cottage had stood at that location for more than sixty years. The original owner was Bertha Eckersley, and upon her death it passed to her daughter, Mary-Jane Evans. Despite its prime city location, after the cottage was demolished, the land remained vacant for decades. A dispute between the city council and the developers meant the issue had dragged through the courts without resolution for years.

Saunders skimmed the next two pages eager to get to the summary. The forensic pathologist determined the bones were at least one hundred years old but were not Aboriginal. He also concluded the bones belonged to females aged between twenty and forty. The final paragraph of the report said they probably had an unfortunate ending, but bone deterioration made that determination inconclusive for all but two of the victims.

Sighing, Saunders put the report into a separate file titled 'Not finalised'. The perpetrator was long dead but with major advances in DNA testing there was a chance the victims could be identified. While there was no designated homicide squad in South Australia in the late nineteenth century, missing people were documented. Not all but some. While many of the old records were now digitally recorded, the task could still be long and laborious.

Saunders liked to get to the crux of the matter quickly, so he was not fond of long and laborious.

He threw his empty coffee cup into the bin by his desk. Whether an investigation, protracted or otherwise, was worth the effort was his next consideration. He had to weigh up the pros and cons. Believing the families of every victim deserved closure, he considered it improbable more than a century later any close relatives of the East Terrace deceased were still alive. However, if living relatives existed, their DNA could help identify the victims.

But there was no need for a hasty decision. The victims had been dead for well over one hundred years so another week or two would make no difference.

Saunders would sleep on it.

About the Author

David Ahern was born, raised and educated in Adelaide, Australia. His first job was at the Adelaide News, a daily newspaper, where he spent eight years as a journalist including two years as the paper's Melbourne correspondent. He then became a news broadcaster on Melbourne radio. A series of jobs followed in government, the public service and in education, writing and editing various publications. He has two adult children and is a supporter of the Adelaide Crows Football Club in the Australian Football League.

Please visit: https://davidbahern.com/

www.ingramcontent.com/pod-product-compliance
Lightning Source LLC
Chambersburg PA
CBHW070553120726
47909CB00007B/2329